Saboteur

a novel

KEVIN MURPHY

GRANITE HOUSE BOOKS

Saboteur
Copyright © 2024 Kevin Murphy

This book is a work of fiction, blending real people and events
from history with fictional characters and storyline. Any
references to historical events, real people, or real places are
used fictitiously. Other names, characters, places and events are
products of the author's imagination, and any resemblance to
actual events, places or persons, living or dead,
is entirely coincidental.

Published by Granite House Books, 2024

Editing and book design by David W. Edelstein
Cover image by Canva Magic Media

ISBN (paperback): 978-1-7382323-0-7
ISBN (ebook): 978-1-7382323-2-1

For my brother Greg,
whose encouragement and enthusiasm
always energize me.

1

6 December 1917. Halifax.

DEATH WAS LURKING IN THE FOG OF HALIFAX HARBOUR.

A little after 8 AM the *Mont Blanc* had slowly emerged from the harbour fog surrounding George's Island. She had arrived in Halifax the day before, too late in the day to be allowed to enter the harbour. The submarine gates that protected the city from German U-boat attacks had already been closed. The ship had to remain outside the gates until early in the morning.

Captain Aimé Le Médec and harbour pilot Francis Mackey had been overly cautious in maintaining a very slow speed along the harbour route to Bedford Basin. They had kept a keen lookout for any shipping activity that might pose a hazard to the *Mont Blanc*.

They were only too aware of the deadly cargo the *Mont Blanc* was carrying. TNT, picric acid and a deck overloaded with barrels of benzene lashed to the railings. All dangerous explosives, especially the picric acid, which was unstable and highly combustible. A collision would be catastrophic.

And yet, no one along the harbour route was aware that the *Mont Blanc* was a floating bomb and posed a danger to all other shipping in the busy harbour. There was not even the mandatory red flag flying to signal that the ship was carrying ammunition.

During its journey towards Bedford Basin the *Mont Blanc*

encountered miscommunications, disregard for harbour protocol, outright bad luck, and a near miss with the Norwegian ship *Imo*.

The near miss was greeted with jubilation and relief.

"Thank God," shouted Mackey, as the two ships came to a standstill.

It was a short-lived euphoria. Although the *Imo* had come to a full stop after the near miss, its momentum carried it forward towards the *Mont Blanc*'s starboard bow, where it rammed the French ship with a piercing shriek of tearing metal. As the *Imo* tried to reverse back out of the collision, its bow anchor, ensnarled in the wreckage, tore out a section of the Mont Blanc's plating, with disastrous results. The *Mont Blanc* was now burning fiercely as it drifted into the main shipping channel.

It was approaching 9 AM on this busy market day in Halifax. To Le Médec's horror the Halifax shoreline was jammed with people. The burning ship was a spectacle that everyone wanted to watch. The crowd even cheered with each barrel of benzene that was lofted into the air with a muffled puff. Great entertainment.

"My God," shouted Le Médec. "We've got to warn them! They've no idea how much danger they're in. Can't we warn them?"

"I can't see how it would be possible, Captain." Francis Mackey shouted. "There's no red flag to indicate we have ammunition aboard. All they see is a burning ship, and they've seen plenty of those burn themselves out without exploding."

"There must be some way of warning them. There's got to be!"

"Captain, we've no way of communicating with anyone on shore. We've a megaphone, but the sound wouldn't reach them."

The crew was now frantic. They were astonished that the *Mont Blanc* had not already exploded, but they also knew what was about to happen. The main deck was starting to heat up, and they were well aware of what lay below those plates. They could see the approaching fire boats coming to the rescue, a rescue they knew wouldn't happen.

Sailors along the starboard rail of the *Mont Blanc* started desperately waving at the fire boats. They were yelling in French—*Get away! Danger!*—but the sailors on the fire boats couldn't hear them and wouldn't have understood what they were saying anyway. They only saw the flailing arms of the *Mont Blanc* crew as a plea for help.

Le Médec cried, "Where's my First Officer? Where's Glotin? Tell him I need some men to lower the anchor so we don't drift closer to shore."

Glotin rushed to the captain. He moaned, "Sir. Sir. We tried to, but the fire was too intense. We couldn't get anywhere near the capstan to lower the anchor. The heat was unbearable."

Le Médec seemed to hang his head as if he was praying to God to intervene. Waiting for an answer and only seeing an abyss.

He thought of his wife. His family. Christmas at home back in France. If he couldn't save the people on shore, he could at least save his crew.

"Abandon ship." He would stay. It was his duty.

The *Mont Blanc*'s life boats had been lowered to launch position as soon as they had left New York. A precaution in the event of a U-boat attack. It took only a matter of minutes for the entire crew to fill the life boats.

Le Médec insisted on remaining with the ship. Mackey couldn't fathom why the captain would choose that obligation. He saw the First Officer, Glotin, rush back up the ladder from the main deck and confront Le Médec. He didn't understand their conversation because it was in French, but whatever Glotin said to the captain worked, because both men descended the ladder and were the last to board the remaining life boat.

The crew rowed with desperation to reach the safety of the Dartmouth shore. They were the only souls prepared for the worst. Only a miracle could save the doomed city.

2

1916. Halifax.

IN 1916, PEOPLE IN HALIFAX DIDN'T BELIEVE THERE WERE German spies and saboteurs actively working in their city. Even though Canada, as part of the British Empire, was at war with Germany, there wasn't active resentment against Germans living and working in their city. There were rumours of active German spies plotting nefarious deeds in and around the great port city, but nothing ever became of these rumours. They just lurked in the background of everyone's daily life, much like religion did.

The citizens of Halifax were more concerned with attacks from German submarines and German bombers. After all, what targets did Halifax have that would draw the attention of saboteurs? There weren't any manufacturers that made explosives and ammunition. Those were the targets that saboteurs went after in the United States. Ammunition depots like Black Tom in New Jersey, blown to bits in the summer.

Surely Halifax wasn't a target for saboteurs. Was it?

$$\underline{3}$$

6 November 1917. North Atlantic.

HE LOOKED LIKE A PHOTO OF JOSEPH CONRAD. HIS EYES were alert and exuded intelligence. His face was framed with a neatly trimmed dark beard and a full mustache that added to his serious expression. His beard almost seemed too large for his face. He was short at five foot three, and never topped the scale over 125 pounds. His dark eyes gave off a certain weariness, as if he had an underlying mistrust for strangers. Maybe that was just shyness. His bearing was erect, revealing the posture of someone with a military background. The only uniform he ever wore was his single-breasted navy-blue sea captain's coat. A coat with two rows of brass buttons and a tightly buttoned neck.

In the dim light of the *Mont Blanc*'s wheelhouse, he stood before the two large rectangular windows that seemed to him like unblinking eyes staring at a grey sky and a pewter ocean. The frothy waves of the Atlantic Ocean delivered a salty mist to the glass in front of his face. *Three days yet to New York*, he thought, *and then what?*

He had no idea that his cargo would consist of highly explosive ammunition. All he knew was that the French government was in dire need of any war supplies they could get their hands on that would help the war effort. He knew his duty and that of the crew, and that was to serve the nation. He firmly believed it was his noble obligation.

We will find out about our cargo soon enough, he thought to himself. Then, on to Halifax to join a convoy leaving on a very dangerous crossing of the Atlantic Ocean back to Bordeaux. He knew there would be British escorts to protect the navel convoy leaving Halifax in early December, but

what if his speed was too slow to keep up with the main body of ships? He would have no choice but to lag behind, a ripe target for the German U-boats.

At 39 years of age, Captain Aimé Le Médec had been at sea for sixteen years, and a captain for two. This was his first voyage aboard the *Mont Blanc*. He was still not completely familiar with its workings. Most of his 39 crew members belonged to the merchant navy and spoke little English. They were all pledged to obey his command and do their duty as required.

4

15 May 1916. New York.

WALTER SCHEELE WAS A LIEUTENANT IN THE GERMAN army until he immigrated to the United States in 1890. A native of Cologne, he had earned a doctorate in chemistry and pharmacology from the university of Freiburg and remained on the payroll of the Imperial War Department as an intelligence officer well after his immigration to America. With the help of German financing, he opened up and ran a successful pharmacy in Brooklyn. He met and married an American woman and led a peaceful life as a neighborhood pharmacist for almost twenty years.

By 1915 he was balding with a fringe of grey hair, but he still carried himself erect like the military man he once was. People saw him as a quiet, reserved man, always seeming to be preoccupied with deep thought. He was a heavy drinker and smoker, which he attributed to his wife's domineering and belittling behaviour.

Between 1912 and 1914, Scheele worked on projects for the Bayer Chemical Company. During this same time, he also worked on creating high explosives for the German military at his secret laboratory in Hoboken, New Jersey. In January 1915 he was instructed by the German government, through its embassy in New York, to make chemical bombs.

*　　*　　*

Franz von Rintelen was a captain in the German army. He had a smooth oval face, a high forehead, light blue eyes and light blonde hair. A model of Aryan manhood, his ramrod straight posture emphasized his military bearing. In April 1915 von Rintelen was ordered to New York to report to the German consulate. He travelled using a Swiss passport under the name of Emile Gache. He was greeted by Franz von Papen, the German military attaché stationed at the German

Embassy in Washington. Von Papen also ran the local secret service on behalf of the German government, a spy network of German agents that were active in an undeclared war against the United States.

Von Papen informed von Rintelen, "You will soon be meeting with a very important person. A pharmacist. In Hoboken. He will be very useful for your purposes, Mr. von Rintelen." Von Rintelen would be funded directly by the German government. His mission was to sabotage American ships carrying munitions and supplies to the Allies.

Later that month von Rintelen met with Scheele in New Jersey. Scheele showed him a four-inch glass tube pipe. It was the same width and length as a cigar. A slim copper disk had been inserted into the middle of the tube, dividing the tube into two equal halves. One end of the tube could be filled with sulfuric acid and the other end with picric acid, and then both ends sealed with wax or tin. The copper disc, Scheele instructed, could be varied in thickness to accommodate the length of time required for the sulfuric acid to eat its way through the copper disc. In effect, a time bomb.

"I can give you a one-day fuse or as much as a seven-day fuse. Whatever length of time you require. All you need to do to arm the device is to pull this tab and the sulfuric acid will begin its work. Once it reaches the picric acid this bomb will create a terrific explosion. More powerful than you can imagine. Just think: a ship leaves New York and explodes five days after it left port." He said this with the pride of a creator.

Von Rintelen realized this was a very powerful weapon that could easily be hidden and remain undetected until it exploded. Dock workers could carry these concealed bombs in their pockets and plant them surreptitiously as they went about their work loading cargo.

5

10 May 1904. Halifax.

RUBEN (BEN) STENDT WAS BORN IN THE CITY OF DANZIG in 1882 to a family with a long German linage. His father had been a fairly successful grain merchant in this wealthy port city, which was part of the Prussian Kingdom. Ruben was the family's only child. Life was comfortable for the Stendt family until the late 1890s, when a crippling depression raged in Prussia and throughout Europe. By the end of the century the family business was suffering and on the point of collapse.

In 1902, the Stendt family finances were in such dire straits that, like hundreds of thousands of others, Otto and his wife Inga immigrated to North America. They arrived in Halifax on 10 May, leaving Ruben behind to finish his military training. He still had two years remaining before he completed his military service. There would be a home waiting for him in Halifax if he ever decided to join them in Canada.

With Otto's qualifications and contacts back in Danzig, he was well qualified to become an agent for the Prairie Wheat Company at their Canadian regional office on Lower Water Street in Halifax. He had a leg up on the other Canadian agents because he was fluent in German and Polish, and he personally knew most of the contacts back in Europe. It wasn't the same as owing your own business, but it was decent employment.

Nova Scotia had welcomed a large number of Germans immigrating to North America during the past 25 years, including a great many who settled in the Annapolis Valley and some who founded their own town, now called New Germany. They were considered hard working people, and assimilated easily into the general population. Mostly they were farmers and carpenters, but many ended up in Halifax, especially those with skills, like cabinet makers, and professionals like doctors and pharmacists. Otto easily fit into the Haligonian population and was welcomed by its German-Canadian citizens.

*   *   *

Although Otto was a successful salesman and a skillful entrepreneur, he had a deadly addiction to the bottle. A year and a half after he and Inga had settled in Halifax, Inga ran off with another man. Down to "*THE U S OF A,*" as Otto would often lament to his wounded pride and to anyone else within earshot. Back in Prussia, when Ruben received his father's letter with his bitter news, he wasn't surprised at what his mother had done. He understood why she would be attracted to someone who really cared for her, but he was deeply wounded that she had deserted him while he still needed her.

Ruben finished his military training in March of 1904, six months before he immigrated to Canada. He had spent five years being groomed as an officer in an elite artillery battalion and was considered a well-disciplined soldier and future officer. He was tall and lean, and always carried himself as a military person. His eyes were cold and his stare could wither a more subservient man, but he projected the authority of a natural born leader.

On a personal basis, he was not the friendliest man to be

around. He did not have many close friends, and those he did associate with for a night at the pub were always deferential to him. Even the short romances he had were not easy-going affairs, and often ended in bitter separations. No one, it seemed, could bear a long relationship with someone who always needed to be in control.

Ruben was honorably discharged from the Prussian army in 1904, when he was 22. The Kingdom of Prussia was part of the German Empire, and a new European war was looming. Moreover, Poland was putting increasing pressure on Prussia for the return of the free port of Danzig to Polish sovereignty. Ruben had had enough of military life, and the thought of being ruled by Poland convinced him he did not have a future in his native city. A more comfortable life beckoned to him from Canada. As soon as his discharge from the Prussian army was finalized, he immigrated to Canada to join his father in Halifax.

When Ruben arrived in Halifax in the summer of 1904, his father had been working for the Prairie Wheat Company for two years and enjoyed a comfortable living serving as the senior agent, dealing with customers back in Prussia. Upon his arrival in Halifax, Ruben moved into the saltbox house that Otto had purchased before his wife had left him.

A saltbox house was a common construction in Halifax, and this one was located in the Richmond neighbourhood, an area in the north end of the city. It had an unimpeded view straight across the Narrows, where the harbour was pinched by the shores of Halifax and Dartmouth before it flowed into Bedford Basin. And it was within walking distance of the waterfront, directly downhill from the house.

By early fall, Ruben had found steady work as a stevedore on the Halifax waterfront. There was no shortage of work for those who were willing to bend their backs and put in their time. It didn't hurt that Ruben's father had a few handy contacts in the import/export trade whose cargos provided lots of employment for stevedores. Being a natural leader, Ruben often found himself in charge of work gangs loading and unloading the many ships passing through Halifax Harbour.

Life seemed to be going well for both father and son until the beginning of the Great War. Otto continued to prosper with the Prairie Wheat Company, but his drinking was becoming a point of friction with his son. Soon after he had begun working on the waterfront, Ruben started calling himself Ben. He wasn't ashamed of his ancestry, but he preferred people to think of him as just another local trying to earn a living. He just didn't want to call attention to his German background. Another contentious issue with his father. Ruben, now Ben, rose in the ranks of the stevedores and gained the respect, if not the friendship, of his fellow dockworkers. He remained a loner and his coworkers let him be.

On a cold, snowy night in late January 1914, Otto had come out of his favourite pub, the Pig's Revenge, where he had drunk more than his normal amount of beer and several Schnaps nightcaps. Maybe it was because of the heated argument he had had with two English sailors about Germany being at fault in starting the war. Witnesses who saw him leave the pub shortly after eleven described him as drunk and unsteady on his feet.

No one knew why he ended up walking along the pier on such a cold, windy night, nor could the police explain how he fell into the harbour. Maybe it was because he was wobbly on his feet and slipped on an ice patch. There was no suspicion of foul play, and the final police report stated he died of misadventure.

6

15 March 1916. Halifax.

HARRY FROBISHER HAD JUST TURNED 33 WHEN HE PASSED all his exams and was promoted to Detective. It certainly didn't hurt his career that his wife, Liz, came from one of the wealthiest families in the South End. The Baldwins.

His Majesty, Donald Baldwin, full of gravitas to the point that he was a caricature of it, was completely in control of his family, and also in control of the Mayor of Halifax, it would seem. He was also a close personal friend of Archbishop Hays, who was among the most influential in Halifax's Catholic community. Donald was just shy of six feet, with a sturdy lean body, and he sported a very bushy white mustache—much fuller than Teddy Roosevelt's, as he liked to point out.

He was originally from Cork, Ireland, where his father was one of the largest landowners in the county. In 1847, which came to be known as Black 47, the Potato Famine had crippled the Irish economy, forcing more than a million people to flee the country. That exodus included the Baldwins, who immigrated to Halifax along with a bundle of family money. Donald was six years old.

The Baldwin family prospered in their adopted home and eventually owned a thriving fish market. By the time Donald inherited it, Corktown Fish Market, located on the best piece of real estate on the Halifax waterfront, was the largest fish market in the Maritimes. It not only catered to the everyday Joes, but was the go-to place for seafood celebrations for wealthy South End Haligonians.

Although there were an equal number of Catholics and Protestants in Halifax, Catholics like Donald seemed to be more equal than the Protestants when it came to political power.

Donald's five children and his wife had lots of family discussions on religion and politics, and never had a falling out over any subject under discussion. However, the second youngest, Peter, seemed to carry around a mild resentment that he had somehow been coerced into becoming a priest; the old Catholic tradition was that every family was blessed if it could provide a son for the priesthood.

Harry was a Sunday Catholic who would never question religious opinions that his wife sometimes used in arguments. Any opposition she had to her father's righteous indignation was as good as non-existent. Growing up, Harry and his friends had often joked about how Protestants were nice, but they weren't going to heaven. Donald would not have found that funny.

Harry had been with the police force since he was 21. He had graduated from high school and spent a year at Dalhousie University, against his parent's wish that he should go to Saint Mary's for the Catholic environment. *Propaganda I don't need*, thought Harry. Then on to the police training academy.

Harry loved his job.

7

31 March 1916. Halifax.

TWO YEARS AFTER HIS FATHER'S DEATH, BEN (NO LONGER Ruben) was still living in the saltbox house. On this particular Friday, two years after the start of World War I, Ben found himself at the Pig's Revenge. March was always an awful month in Halifax. Sometimes there was a hint of warm weather, but mostly it was wet with bone-chilling temperatures. And depressing, because it seemed that winter would never end. It had been like this for the last week, with no end in sight. "I wonder if it is like this in Danzig today?" Ben said to his two companions, Peter and Edward. It had been a busy day on the docks, and the three of them had spent a good part of the afternoon loading heavy skids of machinery onto a freighter bound for France. *War goods to be used against our old homeland*, thought Ben with some bitterness.

Like Ben, Peter had anglicized his name, too. It was much easier for Englishmen to say than Pieter, and it sounded close to his real name. The other man, Horst, he had made a complete change, now calling himself Edward. Both had been born in Canada, Peter in New Germany and Edward in Lunenburg. Neither one had strong feelings about Germany's role in the war.

They were enjoying their Friday night out with their work mates to celebrate Ben's promotion to supervisor. They didn't exactly think of Ben as a warm and friendly guy, but he stood up to management whenever there was an issue affecting their well-being. Like the time Peter had gotten into a fist fight with a second mate on a French freighter who then threatened to have Peter fired over the incident.

"Well, I don't know about the weather in Danzig," ventured Peter, "but I can tell you it's colder than a witch's tit here. They got any witches in Danzig?"

Ben laughed, "No witches. But they've got mighty fine German beer there. Not that there is anything wrong with Oland's, but it just ain't German beer. And I can tell you, you haven't ever tasted bratwurst and sauerkraut like you get back in the old country."

Edward piped up, "I can see that you miss all of those good things from back home, but my parents have made a good life here in Nova Scotia, and together with a lot of other German immigrants we have done a pretty good job of maintaining our culture here in this very fine country. I know a place down in New Germany where you can get real German beer and real German sausage. You would swear you were back in Danzig."

"Tell me Edward, how do you feel about living in Canada, a country that is at war with Germany?" Ben didn't want to get into a long and tedious discussion about German immigrants and their loyalty to Canada, but he did want to gauge their feelings for Germany in this European war. He was more interested to know if they would root for Germany, even if they wanted to hide their true feelings from their fellow citizens.

"Canada is only at war with Germany because they are part of the British Empire. They should have stayed neutral like the Americans. Peter agrees with me."

"I do," whispered Peter, "but I don't think it's something we should talk too loudly about. We may have a German ancestry, but most of the people in this country have an English or Irish or

Scottish ancestry. I think we would all be wiser to consider ourselves Canadians first and be done with it."

"One thing we don't have to worry about, and that is conscription," grunted Ben. "If the Canadian government passes the conscription act like they are threatening to do, things could get very ugly if they try and draft German immigrants who are Canadian citizens into the Canadian army."

"Do you think that could happen?" asked Peter.

Ben answered, "I think the conscription bill will be passed, but not anytime soon. The French Canadians in Quebec are so strenuously opposed to it, and their protests are becoming violent to the point the federal government keeps dragging their feet on this legislation."

Because conscription had not been introduced, the Canadian military relied solely on volunteers to fill its ranks. There was a general feeling in the country, especially in Quebec, that this was Britain's war. While most of the population cheered for Britain, many didn't want to fight in a European war.

8

1916. New York.

PAUL KOEING WAS A GERMAN-AMERICAN AND A FORMER security chief for the Hamburg America Line. His oval face was crowned with long black matted hair that he kept in place with loads of grease. And he had an enormous belly. He was fearsome in his apprehension of robbers who plied their trade against the German passenger company. He had been very well-known to Franz von Papen, who ran the local secret service on behalf of the German government. No one was more suited than Koeing to manage the day-to-day operations for von Papen's secret service.

In 1915 von Papen had been recalled to Germany at the request of the United States government, after being implicated in cases of espionage and sabotage. His secretary, Wolf von Igel, became von Papen's successor and continued to run the German spy ring until he too was arrested, in April 1916.

Paul Koeing continued his activities and stayed in close contact with Wolf von Igel.

One of Koeing's most loyal recruits was a man who worked as a clerk at the National City Bank of New York. Frederick Scheindl handled telegrams from Allied countries transmitting for the purchase of war materials. Often, these telegrams listed the vessels carrying cargo into New York Harbour, but as well, listed the ships that would be carrying it out.

*   *   *

Danny Sullivan, a familiar resident within the Irish community of New Jersey, was a 29-year-old immigrant from Dublin who often found himself out of work, drifting from boarding-house to boarding-house. He had an Irish face, round with red cheeks, curly ginger hair and two angled slashes of ginger that served as eyebrows and gave his face a perpetual frown.

Sullivan had immigrated from Dublin in 1907 when he was twenty years old. There were rumours that he had had some affiliation with the IRA before he immigrated, but that may have been nothing more than a whisper campaign started and spread by Sullivan himself. He had, however, been an active participant in the Irish Home Rule movement that campaigned for self-government and independence from Great Britain. It was the dominant political movement of Irish nationalism from 1870 to the end of World War I.

Growing up in a family with strong views for independence, Danny Sullivan gravitated to those who voiced the same views as he did, and often talked about doing something violent against the English colonialists. By the time he was eighteen, Sullivan was part of a group of patriots who wanted to plant a bomb somewhere in central Dublin to show their support for home-rule. Although this group had no support from the IRA they decided to act anyway.

The bomb exploded in a trash container near the entrance to the oldest pub in Ireland, the Brazen Head, and killed a woman and her three-month-old child. Sullivan did not take part in the actual bombing, but he was implicated just by being a known member of the group. His parents knew of his involvement with this group and worried that their son would be killed by the English militia. They urged him to move to New York for his own safety.

When the war started, Sullivan was well entrenched in New York's shabbier social strata. He was slow-witted and gullible, and habitually repeated other people's arguments as his own. He was quite vehement about his hatred for the British, so it was no surprise that he often championed Germany and openly expressed his desire to help that country in their war effort. Not that he was alone in these feelings, but his anti-American vitriol often landed him in hot water in his bitter arguments with other pub patrons, all of them having too much to drink.

It was his pro-German sentiments, but especially his anti-American ravings, that finally attracted the attention of Paul Koeing.

9

7 November 1917. North Atlantic.

IT WAS A VERY WINDY MORNING, WITH SPITTING SPRAY streaking the two large windows of the *Mont Blanc*'s wheelhouse with salty brine. The kind of day you needed a sturdy pair of sailor's legs to keep from being tossed about. Aimé and his wheelsman, Alphonse, sheltered in the lee of the wheelhouse under a metal overhang. They were buttoned up tight against the icy cold. Alphonse blew a cloud of smoke from his hearty lungs; it was immediately shredded by an angry gust of wind.

"Well, Aimé, two more days before we dock in New York. I am not looking forward to that."

"Neither am I, Alphonse."

"So, your maiden voyage as captain! In the confusion of leaving port, I never got to offer you my congratulations for your promotion. So, I'm offering them now."

"Thank you, my friend. We've known each other for a long time, and it is my great pleasure to be sailing together with you again."

The *Mont Blanc* lurched to port as a large passing wave carved a sudden hole in the ocean. The two men seemed oblivious to the jolt after so many years at sea.

"Tell me Alphonse, what do you think of this ship? It seems a bit sluggish to me."

"It's that all right, but it will do the job. I'm sure the government is confident of that."

Aimé wasn't so sure of that. The French government knew that the *Mont Blanc*'s two sister ships, the *Antilles* and the *Abd el-Kader*, were better maintained and were much faster ships. He wondered why they had not been commissioned for this mission. He figured out in his own mind that those ships were needed urgently somewhere else and the *Mont Blanc* would just have to do. He had no idea at this time what the *Mont Blanc*'s cargo would be. All he did know was that he would be joining a British convoy out of Halifax sometime in early December.

"Well, as long as our cargo doesn't weigh us down too much, we should be able to keep up with the rest of the ships leaving Halifax next month. It will certainly be nice to be back in Bordeaux. I am looking forward to spending Christmas with my family. I have been promised a few days leave when we return."

"That's a nice reward to be looking forward to. Your lovely wife and four beautiful children. Christmas dinner. I envy you, Aimé. My wife has been gone for nearly eight years now. And my only son is serving somewhere on the western front."

"What will you do at Christmas?"

"For the most part I'll be staying with the ship. If the fates allow, I'll have Christmas dinner with my sister and her family. They live just outside of Bordeaux, in the little village of Cestas."

"If God is good to us that will all come to pass. I will be glad when this awful war is over. I cannot understand completely why it ever started in the first place. Let's go inside and get a bit warmed up."

10

9 April 1916. Halifax.

SUNDAY DAWNED BRIGHT AND SHINY, LIKE A NEWBORN baby claiming a fresh start to a brand-new waiting life. Harry and Liz had often been invited to attend mass at St. Mary's Basilica with Liz's parents and then head back to their place afterwards for an early dinner.

Today her brother Peter, the priest, would be joining them. St. Thomas Aquinas, over near the North West Arm, was his home parish. He had a room in the glebe house, where he also took his meals. Having home-cooked roast beef with his family was always a welcome change. A nice day would also give him a good excuse to pedal over to Tower Road. Flat and level almost the whole way.

Donald and Margaret Baldwin lived on Tower Road near the golf club. It was also close to Point Pleasant Park, and if they finished dinner by two o'clock Harry and Liz would have time for a stroll in the park. After all, it was a gorgeous spring day, too nice to waste.

The two eldest Baldwin children were both happily married and immersed in their very busy lives. *Too busy to come for a Sunday dinner after mass*, Donald often thought with some bitterness. Margaret often had to remind him that their children had families of their own, and taking care of their young children was a time-consuming job. Each family had two children apiece, with one more on the way.

Margaret was a stoic. She looked strong and quite capable of bearing another four children herself if that had been God's will. Her role now was to oversee her grandchildren's upbringing, much to the annoyance of both her daughters, who tried to keep Granny's influence in the background. That wasn't easily done, and it sometimes caused some friction in the Baldwin household. Liz's daughter, Mildred, was a mild-mannered child, and she sometimes felt caught in the middle of Granny's strong Catholic views and her parents' more relaxed attitudes toward religion.

Donald (never Don) was the consummate patriarch. He looked like a caricature of an Irishman. He had red apple cheeks, round, suspicious eyes and a bushy white mustache. He looked like someone who was always in charge, whether to his wife or his business partner, Arthur. After Donald's father had passed away, Arthur had joined him as an equal partner in running the Corktown Fish Market. The prosperous fish store had made both partners quite wealthy.

Harry wore a summer suit for the first time. His Sunday suit. It was a nice dark blue and he complimented it with a white shirt and a polka-dot bow tie. And of course, his summer fedora, like every other man in the city wore. At least the gentler class of people.

The three Frobishers arrived in the church parking lot, with fifteen minutes to spare before the eleven o'clock service. Harry, Liz and their seven-year-old daughter, Mildred. They had recently started calling her Milly. Harry hadn't been to confession for a couple of months, and although he should not take communion because of that fact, he knew that people would notice his absence at the communion rail and snicker to their partners that Harry must have some heavy-duty sins to abstain from holy communion.

Not to mention a likely sarcastic comment from Donald after mass. So, he reluctantly took the wafer.

Roast beef for dinner on Sunday afternoon was something of a ritual, and Harry always enjoyed it. Peter, his brother-in-law, could sometimes be a bit of a pill, but today he seemed to be in a jovial mood. Ordinarily he seemed to carry a chip on his shoulder because he felt that it was his burden to be the sacrificial son offered to the priesthood. Harry thought he would have been happier if he had joined the police force because he had a naturally inquiring mind.

"I was wondering," Peter said to Harry, "if you think there are German saboteurs plotting mischief here in Halifax? I mean, you being a detective and all. Do you ever have to investigate any rumours or suspicious individuals?"

"For sure, there are rumours. But none I have investigated that bore any fruit. To tell you the truth, the prevailing attitude in the city is that we are going to be bombed by a German bomber. Even a submarine attack seems more likely than a German agent attacking a target around here."

"Yes, I probably agree with you. But still, we have a lot of Germans living here. Don't you think those citizens arouse any suspicion?"

Donald spoke up. "Most of those Germans have been here for years. Many came in the wave of German immigrants in the late 1800s. They were great farmers and they had an excellent work ethic. I am confident they feel as Canadian as any of us. They left their homeland for a better life here, and I think they feel that this is their country now."

"But still," Liz interjected, "their roots are German so they must have some deep-down sympathies for Germany, regardless."

"Maybe so," said Donald," but they have invested a lot of

hard work in building a good life here. I don't think they want to jeopardize it. I think Harry is right. Most Haligonians probably believe that we will be attacked directly by Germany rather than by home-grown saboteurs. Most of the people I meet in the fish business who are of German descent seem like hard working people. I personally have no suspicions. I am sure Harry would warn us if we need to be concerned."

Peter replied, "I guess so. If Harry was hiding information from us, it would be like he was lying to us, and that would be a sin and he wouldn't be able to take holy communion. But he did take it today, so I guess we should feel safe."

"I guess, Peter, being a priest, you have to bring religion into this, although I know you are being facetious. But it's good to see you being light about religion. On the ..."

"Harry! We don't want to get into a religious discussion. Do we!" Liz was adamant.

11

29 April 1916. New York.

BEN LIKED HIS LIFE IN CANADA. AFTER ALL, HE HAD LIVED in Halifax for twelve years, and he was proud of his Canadian citizenship. Although he was also proud of his German heritage, he had no reason to emigrate back to his native Danzig. And do what, enlist in the Germany army? Again?

He had no grudge against his adopted country, but he did hate the Americans for supplying Germany's enemies with ammunition that would be used against his old homeland. The bloody Americans, who were supposed to be neutral.

He also thought about the German saboteurs working in the United States. *Weren't they fighting a secret war against America by blowing up armament factories and infecting horses being sent overseas with anthrax?* He cheered for them, but it was a secret cheer. He would never give anyone the scantest reason to suspect where his true sympathies lay.

Although he was just 34, his full head of closely cropped black hair was laced with grey. He was tall, with menacing blue-grey eyes, definitely was not someone you would want for an enemy. His stare could penetrate you like a saber. He was someone you could imagine as an army lieutenant, someone you would follow into battle.

Unmarried and certainly not domesticated, Ben preferred the company of casual girlfriends and the occasional comfort he paid for at his favourite brothel. He was a bachelor simply because he was not married. He wasn't queer. Just unmarried and a confirmed bachelor. It was widely believed that bachelors had no domestic skills—that they didn't know how to cook, or sew, or iron, or clean a house. Those were women's duties, and men needed women to look after these things. Conventional wisdom, perhaps, or just people's assumption. But none of this mattered to Ben. He could take care of himself, and in any case he just preferred to live on his own.

He had inherited his father's house up in the Richmond area of Halifax. It was near the dockyards, and afforded him a comfortable place to live. Plus, it was only a short walk to the waterfront where he had worked as a stevedore for the past twelve years. He could cook, and anyway there were plenty of taverns and restaurants where he could eat. And there were cleaning ladies to tidy up his house and wash his clothes.

Ben often wondered if he should be doing something to aid the efforts of his fellow "soldiers" in New York. Because that is what we are, aren't we? Soldiers for the homeland. We don't wear uniforms, but then again, the people who man the ships carrying war supplies to Britain and France don't wear uniforms, either. After all, those saboteurs are part of an army, an army of support for the enemies of Germany. So, in a sense, they could be considered soldiers as well.

He didn't have any feelings of ill will toward Canada. He knew that the convoy ships that left Halifax were carrying war supplies that would benefit Germany's enemies. War supplies that were manufactured and loaded into ships going to England and France. It was as clear as day that the United States was unequivocally on the side of Britain and France, even though the U.S. had never declared war against Germany.

He thought that if the United States was loose on their neutrality status, he would be within his rights to counter their illegal delivery of war supplies to the enemies of Germany. A private war of two undeclared combatants. His mission was to disrupt the supply lines. He knew that Germany had saboteurs actively working in New York, creating mayhem with stray bomb attacks on American arms manufacturers and ammunition storage depots. He resolved to do something, some action to help disrupt the illegal arms supply to Germany's enemies. Even if he did it on his own, even on a small scale.

Ben had arranged for a two-week vacation beginning on Monday, 24 April. He took a train from Halifax on Saturday morning and arrived in New York early Sunday morning. During that long train ride, he had too much time to stew in his raging thoughts. The fucking Americans. His only goal for this trip was to make contact with the German underground in New York City.

After several hours of inquiry looking for accommodation, he eventually ended up in a boarding house located in the German immigrant neighborhood of Williamsburg. It was run by an older German couple, which was ideal. Perhaps this German emigree population would be a good place to find a contact who could introduce him to someone connected to a secret German underground.

* * *

If Ben came to New York looking for support, he certainly came to the right place. By some estimates, the German population of New York was as much as ten per cent of the eight million people who lived in and around the city. Many of these were first generation immigrants still very much tied to their fatherland. They were a prominent and articulate force within the general population.

In fact, there was a German language newspaper selling 75,000 copies a day. Cities like Hoboken were almost entirely German.

For most of his first week, Ben hung out at waterfront bars and restaurants in German immigrant neighborhoods like Yorkville and Williamsburg. He was aware that most immigrants had arrived in droves in the late 1800s and were often wealthy and skilled artisans. Many weren't. They were working men, stevedores, who competed with the Irish for work and control of employment on the waterfront.

It didn't take Ben long to realize that many locals were still tied to Germany's aspirations and voiced little support for the English cause. He sensed that they were ripe for a chance to aid Germany in the war. Especially since America made no bones about supplying the enemy with war materials.

If he hung out in these neighborhoods, it seemed, sooner or later he would likely meet someone who would help him get in touch with someone who shared his feelings about neutral America helping Germany's enemies. He had tried making inquiries at the German embassy in Washington but they just seemed suspicious of him. They probably thought he was an American spy.

One bar Ben favoured in his search for companionship was the Edelweiss Biergarten over on Grand Street in the Lower East Side. The ceiling in the main room hung low and smoke was the oxygen that everyone breathed. It was a boisterous place where you could get a decent Bratwurst and sauerkraut and listen to the resident accordionist. And meet people who made no pretense of where their sympathies lay. Alcohol had a way of loosening tongues.

He went there most days, sometimes for a bite to eat at lunchtime, but more often in the early evening to drink with whoever was available for conversation. He intentionally made a nuisance of himself by ranting on that he was a German Canadian and how upset he was with how the American government continually favoured Germany's enemies by supplying them with war materials and other supplies while continuing to remain neutral to the war.

He toasted saboteurs whose actions seemed to right this wrong and demonstrated that Germany was not going to take this sitting down. He was vocal in wishing he could do something himself.

It is no surprise that sentiments like that became rumours that circulated widely in the immigrant community.

* * *

Paul Koeing knew every dockworker, sailor and tug captain working on the piers. He knew the rhythms of the harbour and the city. He knew where men hid when they didn't want to be found. He was a man who paid attention to rumours and gossip. It was inevitable that he would hear about a Canadian of German descent who was sniffing out Germans in New York with allegiance to their old homeland.

Franz von Papen had been the original architect who created Germany's secret intelligence network in America. Koeing had been an integral part of that network. Von Papen had been expelled from the United States by the American government last year on grounds of espionage, and his successor had also been expelled just recently.

Franz von Rintelen had not been implicated in either of these events, although he was very much a part of the secret underground. With their expulsions he became the heir to the throne, and had now inherited control of running the agent network.

His mission continued to be the sabotage of American ships

carrying munitions and supplies to the Allies. He worked closely with the chemist, Dr. Scheele, in the design and manufacture of cigar bombs and had a long-standing association with Paul Koeing in the recruitment of agents.

*   *   *

Always on the lookout for dependable people, Koeing made a point of visiting the Edelweiss Biergarten on this Saturday night. He had heard that the Canadian often went there for some companionship and good German beer.

True to the intelligence he had received, he found Ben sitting at a long table with three husky men who had just come off shift and were enjoying being single for a few hours before heading home to the missus. The men were stevedores, just like Ben, so Ben fit right in with their company.

One of the men noticed Koeing sitting alone several tables away and raised his stein in salute. Koeing took that as an invitation and joined the group. The first impression Ben had of Koeing was that of a greasy-looking man with a huge belly that would look right at home wearing a butcher's apron and wielding a large meat cleaver.

Hugo, who was the only one that was familiar with Koeing, made the introductions. "And this here lad is Ruben, although he prefers to be called Ben. He's a Canuck, but he originally hailed from Danzig."

"*Guten abend meine Freunde,*" Koeing said with good cheer. "Thank you for the invitation."

"You're welcome," said Hugo. "We had a long day loading supplies going to France and England. We have worked up quite a thirst."

"Aiding the enemy is what we done," said Schaede, a tall thin man with a bushy mustache. "Even though we love life here in America."

"Might I remind you, Herr Schaede, that we, I mean America, are not at war with Germany," replied his friend Hugo."

"That is definitely so." Koeing said with emphasis. "Formally, America is not at war. More than a million of our forefathers immigrated from Germany in the last century. They have prospered and done well in America. But there is no denying that that German heritage has been forsaken at the expense of America's illegal support for England and France. It is only a pretense that America is not at war with Germany." he said all this with a straight face, knowing full well that Franz von Rintelen was fighting a secret war.

Ben wasn't sure if he should respond, or how he should respond. He didn't know these people well enough to trust them completely. Was it possible that the U.S. government had their own spies lurking here? *But*, he thought, *what the hell, I came here for a purpose so shit or get off the pot. Life is full of risk.*

"I can see your position, Mr. Koeing. And it is different than mine. In Canada we are definitely at war with Germany. We are part of the British Empire, and as such, we choose, as a country, to support England. Canada may have waited a spell to make its own declaration of war, but that was only to show the world that Canada is an independent country, separate from England-that we can make our own decision."

Koeing, thinking he should pay some attention to this Canadian, said, "Good point, Ruben, or should I say Ben. I am betting America will be formally at war with Germany within the next year. Then we shall be in the same position as you."

"I am sure that will be the case. But in the meantime, I would like to do something to support the German war effort. The British navy controls most of the security around the port of Halifax, but they are much less vigilant there than American security is around New York harbour. There are far more incidents in your country that are blamed on German saboteurs than there are in Canada."

An hour later, after a few more steins of beer, most of the group had departed for their homes, leaving Ben and Koeing to themselves. As the beer relaxed him, Ben felt comfortable enough to confide in Koeing more of his intention to sabotage ships leaving Halifax bound for the UK. He again stressed his love for his adopted country, but like the Irish he had no love for Great Britain. He would like to act, but he had no accomplice and he wasn't sure how to start.

"Mr. Koeing…"

"Please Ben, call me Paul. If we are going to continue a relationship we should do so as friends."

12

1 May 1916. New York.

PAUL KOEING HAD SET UP A MEETING WITH FRANZ VON Rintelen at a quiet little café far from the German consulate. It needed to be a discreet meeting, with no possibility of a casual passerby recognizing any personnel from the consulate. Koeing arrived ten minutes late.

"*Guten Morgan*, Herr von Rintelen. Have you ordered breakfast? "He would never dare address von Rintelen as *Franz*. Koeing was much too indoctrinated in social and military discipline to ever treat his superiors as anything other than his superiors.

"Hello Paul. Yes, thank you. I have ordered scrambled eggs, some toast and coffee. I seriously considered a Polish sausage but thought better of it. Maybe you can try one."

"I think I will just have a large coffee. That will do me just fine."

"I gather you are quite receptive to help your new Canadian friend carry out some activities in the port of Halifax, with a little help from our patriots here in New York. Tell me what you know about Ruben, or should I call him Ben?"

Koeing summarized what he knew about Ruben. "He immigrated to Canada in 1904 and has been working on the Halifax waterfront ever since. He inherited his father's house when the old man got drunk one night and fell off a Halifax dock. Proud of his German heritage and likes to rant about the god damn Americans supplying the Allies with ammunition to be used against his old homeland. He is a bit of a hothead, but he manages to keep it under control."

"Do you trust him, Paul? That's what I want to know."

"My instinct says, yes. I do have a contact in Halifax. Someone who works as a clerk in the local newspaper. I called him yesterday and he agreed to do a little research for me. Very discreet research. If he vouches for Ruben, I will give him a trial run."

"So, your gut feeling is to trust him! I respect you Paul, and if you are comfortable using Ruben then I support you."

"His job definitely puts him in a good position to plant our special devices," Koeing said with some confidence. "He is a man with a grudge. I trust him but I don't like him. He is a mean son-of-a-bitch, a real killer if you crossed him. I don't think he would hesitate to kill someone if he got in the way. The thing that bothers *me* is that he could kill anyone who was in his way and it wouldn't bother *him* at all. But that suits our purposes just fine."

"All right. Why don't you take him to see our favourite pharmacist and arrange for a little demonstration. Make sure he learns how to handle those bombs. And especially how to arm them properly. Then you will have to arrange for an initial shipment to Nova Scotia."

"Do you remember that guy, the Irishman, Danny Sullivan?"

"Just what you told me."

"I haven't used him for anything yet. He has some low-level affiliation with the Irish mafia here in New York. I think the association goes back to his days in Ireland. From what I can gather he seems a bit of a loose cannon. But I am thinking that if he had someone to lead him, he could serve as a ready accomplice to someone like Ruben Stendt. I am going to persuade Ruben to use him in Halifax, and if things turn out well, then we may be in business for future missions."

13

8 November 1917. North Atlantic.

THE *MONT BLANC* CRUISED WITH LITTLE EFFORT ON A smooth ocean under a bright blue sky. Its single smokestack emitted a thin white stream of smoke that floated aimlessly into a windless emptiness. Aimé and Alphonse leaned against the rear deck railing that jutted out over the rudder. It gave them an unobstructed view of the endless ocean.

"Tomorrow is the day, Alphonse. With this weather we are making good speed, and we should arrive in New York ahead of schedule."

Alphonse blew out a great lungful of smoke from his well-used pipe, a present from his father many years ago. "Yes, Captain. And then our quiet time aboard this ship will be over. The whole crew will be anxious to finish this voyage, especially if we are carrying any armaments as part of our cargo."

"We'll find that out tomorrow. You know it is our duty, Alphonse, to accept whatever assignment that is handed to us." It was in quiet moments like this that the captain's feelings betrayed a world-weariness, perhaps borne of too many long, lonely days at sea. "I am more worried about the voyage from Halifax to Bordeaux. If the weather is bad and our cargo is overly heavy, we might have to lag behind the convoy if we're unable to keep up."

Alphonse had no doubt that his captain would do his duty.

He had known Le Médec for many years and knew he could be as personable as a saloon-keeper. When he was away at sea, he took his duty seriously, which may have made him seem aloof and moody, but he was a conscientious officer who did things by the book.

14

2 May 1916. New Jersey.

IT WAS A BEAUTIFUL, SUNNY DAY, WITH NOT A CLOUD IN sight. Ben was sitting in Washington Park over by the soccer field. He was eating a bratwurst that he had bought from a street vendor. He wasn't particularly hungry. It was more of a gesture to remind him of home. He was waiting for Paul Koeing.

Last Saturday night, after a good heart-to-heart discussion, they had agreed that they had a common goal. The destruction of ships carrying war supplies to the Allies. A few more rounds of Schnaps cemented their bond.

Koeing had acknowledged that there was no German spy network in Canada. Ben convinced him that Halifax might be a ripe base of operations. Many of the convoys carrying cargos to England and Europe were assembled in Bedford Basin, at the head of Halifax Harbour.

"As you know, Paul, I am a Canadian citizen living in Halifax. Although Canada is at war with Germany, there is not the same resentment toward German immigrants living in Nova Scotia as there is here in New York and New Jersey. I work on the water-front as a stevedore, loading and unloading cargo ships."

"Most of the ships arriving in Halifax are already fully loaded and ready for inclusion in a convoy, are they not?" Koeing asked. "They wouldn't need any stevedore services".

"True, and it certainly limits the number of ships we can target." Ben continued. "But there are some ships carrying regular war supplies, like grain, coal, or even livestock, and they sometimes require additional supplies to be loaded in Halifax. Often, it's food stores for the ocean crossing. Some ships need small repairs, which means they have to berth in one of the dry docks. So, there are opportunities that arise that can be exploited. These softer targets do not have the security that the ammunition ships have, so it's easier to plant a device somewhere in the hold. My mission is to destroy or at least damage some of those ships."

"It doesn't seem that you are going to have a lot of opportunities. Nothing like here in New York"

"That may be so, but there will be some opportunities, however few, and the success of those opportunities will be of value to the German sabotage effort you are conducting in New York."

Ben was ready and looking forward to meeting this mysterious "bomb-maker" when Koeing picked him up a little before eleven. It was a short drive to the pharmacy. They arrived just before noon and were greeted by Walter Scheele.

Scheele looked like a pharmacist. He wore a white lab coat over a dark suit, with a white shirt and a bow tie that looked like it been tied by hand. With a build like FDR, he had a long face and a receding hairline with neatly combed grey hair. He wore round wire spectacles and his face was freshly shaved. He had brown eyes that were set close together and a welcoming countenance. He looked like somebody's uncle, although he was anything but. Future press stories would often refer to him as the "mad bomber."

"Welcome gentlemen. I am pleased to be of service." And he meant it. Maybe there was another outlet for his deadly inventions. The more bombers, the merrier. All for the greater glory of Germany. "Let me invite you to my laboratory for a little demonstration. I understand, Herr Stendt, that you have a burning zeal to help the Kaiser in any way you can. This could be your ticket."

Scheele took them to a shack deep in the woods, a spot far from prying eyes. He showed them one of his cigar bombs and explained how the mechanism worked and how the delayed timer could be activated to ignite in a few hours or a few days. Ben was astonished at how simple the device was. "Ingenious," he exclaimed.

"Here, Ben, hold it in your hand. It is quite safe." He handed him the four-inch tube. Ben was a little nervous at first, but soon felt comfortable handling the device. "That tube you are holding has a copper disc inserted into the middle of the pipe. It is air tight. It divides the tube into two compartments. One compartment is filled with picric acid and the opening is sealed with wax. "Do you know what picric acid is, Ben?"

"I think it's used in explosives, but I really don't much about it."

"You are right. It has varied commercial uses, but it is definitely used in explosives. Bombs. It is flammable and very combustible. It is safe as long as it is sealed in the tube between the wax and the copper plug. However, if it comes in contact with an agent like sulfuric acid it will create quite a detonation. So, it should be no surprise to you that the other end of the tube is filled with sulfuric acid. As you probably know, or should know, sulfuric acid has a corrosive effect on copper."

"You mean, the sulfuric acid eats through the copper plug?"

"Exactly. This little knob in the center of the pipe. It has a stem that separates the sulfuric acid from the copper disc. If you were to pull out this knob right now, the sulfuric acid would start eating away at the copper disc. And when the sulfuric acid reaches the picric acid, the combination will produce a flame as hot as a tiny fragment of the sun."

"That's it!"

"That's it. Almost. There is another basic factor you need to know if you are going to be using any of these devices. You have to know how long it takes the sulfuric acid to eat through the copper disc. It all depends on the thickness of the copper plug. Believe me, I have done extensive testing on this.

"The tube you are holding will explode in about one day from the time you remove the knob. I can vary the thickness of the copper disc so it will explode in three days or six days. So, in effect, this is a time bomb. You plant it on a ship that is leaving port today and the explosion occurs five days later, when the ship is far out to sea."

Ben was ecstatic, and that fervor ignited a burning passion to bring a shipment of these bombs back to Halifax. Little did he know that Scheele's bombs had been used to set fire to the Canadian Parliament buildings a few months earlier, in February.

Koeing was quite delighted at how things had turned out. Putting his hand on Ben's shoulder he said, "Now all we have to do is get a supply of these 'cigars' to you in Nova Scotia. I am thinking longer fuses would suit you better. Maybe four- or six-day fuses. Each tube will be marked with a number indicating the approximate length of time it will take to explode once the tab has been pulled. And… I also have someone to work with you in Halifax. An Irishman. They hate the British as much as Germans do."

15

27 May 1916. Halifax.

TODAY WAS DANNY'S BIRTHDAY. HE WAS 30 YEARS OLD and wanted to celebrate. He had been in Halifax for almost two weeks now. The boarding house on Brunswick Street where he was living was a bit shabby, but it was better than the dive in New York. He still had most of the $500 that Koeing had given him to travel to Halifax.

Koeing had told him to lay low and not to draw undo attention to himself. See if he could get some work on the waterfront. And a place in a boarding house that wouldn't arouse the interest of other boarders. "And for God's sake, don't get drunk and shoot your mouth off about your opinions on the fucking war."

Danny and Ben had met the week before. They met at the Pig's Revenge because it was a public place and usually crowded. Ben was also very familiar with the place and went there on occasion with some of the other stevedores after their shift was over.

It wasn't hard to spot Danny Sullivan with his distinctive curly red hair. He was sitting alone, hunched over a quart of Oland's. Ben's first impression was of a surly disposition. Someone who looked like he had a chip on his shoulder.

Ben took a seat at a nearby table with a fellow worker he had a nodding acquaintance with. "Mind if I join you?"

"Not at all. Ben, isn't it?"

"It is. And I forget your name."

"John. I'm just finishing off this here quart while the wife is shopping. She told me to have a drink and meet her at Eaton's. One drink, she said, and then I could help her carry her shopping bags home."

They didn't really have much to talk about. The weather, of course. And how the war was affecting life in Halifax. John finished his beer and left to meet his wife.

"Would you like some company?" Ben turned sideways and offered a friendly face to Danny. "I'm not a great conversationalist, but I don't particularly like drinking alone. My friend here had to go and meet his wife."

"I'd be glad of the company. Name's Danny. I've only been in town for a short while."

"Just visiting, are you?" Ben moved over to the small table by the window and introduced himself. They were in a small alcove off of the main seating area and had plenty of privacy.

Before Danny had left New York, Koeing had given him Ben's home address. Ben did not have a phone, so Danny had written to him and suggested he would be at the Pig on this particular day. The tavern meeting went well, and the two agreed to meet again very soon.

In the meantime, Ben said, he could probably be of help to get Danny employed as a stevedore on the waterfront. He told Danny he would have to do this discretely, as he didn't want them to know he and Danny were already acquainted. "Rest assured, you will find work there, because I know they are looking for extra help these days."

So, on this particular Saturday night, Danny was not only going to celebrate his birthday. He was also going to celebrate his new job on the waterfront. He was to start on Monday, and while he wouldn't be a stevedore yet, he would be employed as a carpenter's helper until an opportunity became available closer to Ben's work environment.

But tonight, first things first. Some whiskey with a beer chaser. Jameson's if they had it, but that was hardly likely. Then onto a place where he had eaten a couple of times, the Olde English Restaurant. He would have preferred if it had been called the Olde Irish restaurant, but his mouth had been watering for a feast of good old-fashioned fish and chips, so the nationality be damned.

He'd have to watch his drinking. But not overdo it, lest it impede his carnal performance over at Harriet's. He had already made arrangements to see the young girl from the Valley. Her name was Elly, and she still had a good bit of the country girl in her. *A little plump, but she had nice tits*, thought Danny. *I am going to savour this birthday present.*

The night started off at the Pig's Revenge. He sat at a lone table next to the bar. "I don't suppose you have any Jameson?"

"We don't, but we've got some Bushmills. Would you like some of that?"

"Bushmills, for Christ's sake. That Protestant crap." Danny said this with some disgust.

"Canada makes some fine whiskeys. How about one of those?" Bill replied with a flourish. Imported whiskey was hard to come by in these days of "official" prohibition. Jameson was made in the Catholic south of Ireland. Bushmills was distilled in Belfast, in the Protestant north. British territory. Perhaps it had something to do with British influence during wartime that made Bushmills easier to import than its southern rival.

"Nope. I don't think Canada knows how to make whiskey. I'll take the Bushmills. A double. No... make it a triple. No ice or water. And a quart of Oland's to chase it. It's me birthday, after all."

Danny didn't overdo it. Just the one round. Next, he headed over to the restaurant and had a platter of their excellent golden fried fish and chips. Two pieces, because it was his birthday. Deep fried, with homemade tartar sauce. He would have had a Guinness, but the restaurant didn't serve alcohol. Just as well. He wanted to be up for all the pleasure he was imagining.

Harriet's was deep into Sailor Town. Over on Creighton Street. He arrived early with a little bit of a buzz.

"Elly's not here. Her monthly came unexpectedly. She's not available. I saved Rita for you. She's a little older but she's got a hell of a lot more experience than Elly. She's with a client right now, but if you come back in an hour, I will make sure she has a bath and is ready for you. Here's a voucher for two dollars. Down the street, maybe halfway, there's an alley with a lit sign that says, BOSE. There are a lot of coloured guys in there, but it's cozy and the booze is cheap."

Danny went to the place. It was crowded and smoky. About two thirds of the patrons were white guys like himself. There were maybe five women in the place, and they all looked like they lived in the neighbourhood. Definitely not from the South End. Danny found a table near the back of the room and settled in with his usual quart of Oland's.

He was angry with Elly. How dare she spoil his birthday celebration. It didn't matter that it was not Elly's fault that she got her period, but somebody had to be blamed for his disappointment. There were two white guys and a coloured guy sitting at the table next to him, and Danny struck up a conversation. Two beers later, they were engrossed in a spirited argument about the war.

It seemed that the two white guys were off duty merchant seamen from New York who were waiting for sailing orders to leave on a convoy for England. The coloured guy was a local, and he kept ranting about this war being a white man's war. He kept insisting that his life was not going to change no matter which side won.

Keith, one of the white guys, jabbed his finger at the coloured guy, "Listen Garvin, if Germany wins the war do you think the United States is going to sit by and cozy up to the German victors? Canada is part of the British Commonwealth, so if England loses so does Canada. And how do you think that is going affect relations between the United States and Canada? So, I would say that your life will definitely be worse if Germany wins."

Danny was getting pissed. He said to Keith, "It's easy to see your position. Americas claim they are neutral in this war. That they have this great big ocean to protect them from the European conflict. Well, I can tell you they're not neutral."

"Oh!" sputtered Keith, "I haven't heard anything about war being declared between the United States and Germany."

Danny's anger was beginning to rear its ugly head. "Not a declared war. But an undeclared war that's in full swing."

"Hogwash," yelled Keith. "The United States is not at war with Germany. Germany's not an enemy."

Danny couldn't help himself. He abruptly jumped up and banged his fist on the table, spilling his glass of beer. "Do you think it's all right for you Americans to transport supplies to England, Germany's enemy, when you're not at war with Germany?" Some of the beer dripped onto Keith's lap and he pushed the table into Danny's legs.

"What of it?! You a fuckin' kraut or something? Get out of here before I hit ya over the head with this here bottle."

Danny gave him a hard shove, hard enough to push Keith off balance. "Fuck you." Keith managed to grab Danny's sleeve and they both fell over along with all the beer.

The Shore Patrol arrived before any police could be called. Their job was to look after rowdy sailors who got into trouble, before the local police could get involved. BOSE and Harriet's were favourite destinations not only for off duty sailors but also for lots of other merchant seamen who wanted to get dunk and laid. The Shore Patrol patrolled this part of town as their regular turf.

They were burly guys with night sticks, and ended up cracking Danny over the side of the head because he continued to pummel the other guy with a broken chair leg. When the police wagon arrived, they told the officers that they only subdued Danny because he threatened them with the chair leg.

No one was arrested, but they did take down a few names, including Danny's. And they did advise Danny to go to the emergency department at the Victoria General and have his head looked at. He had a deep gash that might need a few stitches. It was definitely not the way Danny had intended to end his birthday celebration.

16

30 May 1916. Halifax.

HARRY FROBISHER ARRIVED EARLY AT HIS DESK ON Tuesday morning. He was supposed to investigate a rumour about a German spy who was planning to destroy one of the submarine nets guarding the harbour entrance. Harry knew it was all a fabrication.

The guy who had called into the switchboard on Monday morning was a known ne'er-do-well who was most likely looking for a handout. He had asked for Harry and told him that he had recently overheard a man with a foreign accent discussing the submarine nets with another shady character in a dark corner of the Pig's Revenge, the most popular tavern in Sailor Town. *Packy O'Leary fancies himself as Harry's secret undercover spy*, Harry had thought as he called him back.

This morning, he was still thinking about that conversation he had had with Packy yesterday, and was pondering what to do when Sandy Wellington intruded on his thoughts. "Good morning, Detective Harry. You are in early today."

"Good morning, Sandy. Or should I call you Sergeant Sandy? How's your leg?"

"Better. I'm going to have all the stitches taken out on Friday."

"They never caught that fucker that shot you, but I'll bet you he won't be showing his face around Halifax anytime soon. If I ever see him around town, I'll shoot him on sight."

"I'll drink to that, Harry."

"Sandy, I have another one of those stupid calls to investigate. Once again, it's a call from Packy. He says he was sitting by his lonesome over at the Pig's Revenge. According to Packy, he was just minding his own business. A whiff of a conversation between two strangers just happens to drift into his consciousness. He thinks he hears an accent he doesn't recognize, and it's got to be a German spy plotting to blow up something. So my man Packy says."

"Well Harry, it *is* 1916. There is a war going on. It wouldn't surprise me to find out that there really are German spies operating here. What about those ammunition plants that keep getting bombed south of the border? And those mysterious ship explosions on convoy ships. Don't you think this the work of your German saboteurs? If these agents are all operating south of the border, who's to say they won't sanction the same operation right here in good old Halifax?"

"I know. You are right. But I can't help feeling I'm wasting my time with these investigations that always turn out to be someone's drunken fantasy."

"Maybe one day you will find out that there are German agents operating here in Halifax. I hope not, but as I say, it wouldn't surprise me."

Harry put on his police overcoat, with the lining removed, and buttoned all the buttons right up to the collar. It was cold and windy, a day that couldn't decide if it should be a day in late Spring or a day in Early summer. The police station was on the lower slope of Citadel Hill, and all that icy harbour wind seemed to funnel directly into the marrow of his bones. He felt it all the way to the heart of Sailor Town.

He had agreed to meet Packy at the Olde English Restaurant at ten o'clock. He knew he would end up buying Packy breakfast but, who knows, Packy might have something useful to say.

"Good morning, governor."

"Fuck the phony British snobbery, Packy. I am not in the mood."

"O.K mate."

"Packy!"

The waitress was a tired looking, worn-out woman who looked like her best years were well behind her. But she was employed, working at a decent establishment, and she was a great asset to the owner of this restaurant. She was the real reason people kept coming here, year after year. People like Harry. Not for the food, which wasn't bad. But for the friendship. Like you'd expect from a familiar bartender.

"Good morning, governor."

"Brenda, if you were a man, I would say something rude to you."

Packy had two eggs, bacon and sausage, beans and buttered toast. And, of course, orange juice and coffee. Harry ordered the same. *Why the hell not!*

"So, Packy, you were over at the Pig."

"As you well know, I frequent the place. Sometimes it takes me an hour to finish a quart of that excellent Oland's Export Ale, but they always leave me alone."

"Tell me about last night."

"There were two guys sitting in the alcove by the back window. No one sits back there because it is too dark. I had to take a leak. The washroom in that place stinks, so I usually go outside to take a piss. If you go out the back door nobody can see you."

"So, these guys weren't paying any attention to you."

"No, they were only interested in their own conversation. While I was relieving myself, I could hear them through the open window. One guy seemed to be doing all the talking, and he had a very strong accent. He sounded German to me, but I figured he was talking to an English person so he had to talk in English.

"What caught my attention was a reference to the submarine nets across the harbour. They were talking about those nets, and while I didn't hear the entire conversation, I heard enough to believe they were talking about destroying them."

"So, you came back inside…"

"I couldn't stay out there holding my dick forever, so I came back inside. Besides, it was fuckin' cold. They were just getting up from their chairs and all I saw was their backs as they left. Oh, and one guy, the shorter one, had very curly reddish hair. It was a very distinctive colour. That, I remember. The other one was taller. He had more of a military bearing."

"That's not much of lead, Packy. It doesn't even seem like a conspiracy. I'm sure lots of people talk about the submarine nets. They may not play a role in everyone's daily life, but they are part of the landscape in Halifax."

"That may be so, Harry, but there was definitely something suspicious about them. Something secretive about their conversation. Call it a gut feeling, if you will. Maybe I don't have any evidence that you could use in court, but I just wanted you to know this as background. I am going to keep an eye out for them."

"Packy, are you sure you didn't just bring me out here for a free breakfast?"

"Naw, Harry. I enjoy your company and breakfast with you is always a pleasure. Especially if the city is paying."

"The city's not paying, Packy."

"In any case, it doesn't hurt to have me as your eyes and ears in places you would never frequent, now does it, Harry? Who knows what I might overhear that would escape official scrutiny?"

"You've got a good point. But I need a little bit more than your hunches, something credible that I can sink my teeth into."

"Deal, Harry."

Packy lived with his old mother on the nicer edge of Sailor Town. He had a girlfriend, Rita, who was a little rough around the edges, but who still managed to entertain clients, usually ones who had had a few and weren't too picky about who they slept with. She was well past her prime, but there was so much demand for her services, it proved the truth of the old saying about how much more attractive women became with every additional drink. And for an old boozer like Packy, she was a cozy companion. The two of them propped each other up and survived.

Rita had been entertaining at Harriet's for well over ten years. She and Harriet were more like old friends than business partners, so Rita had a lot of leeway about when she wanted to work or spend time with her boyfriend. And it wasn't uncommon that Packy stayed over for the night, especially when the evening traffic was light.

Harry knew that Packy was in a position to "overhear" things that his girlfriend might come across in her nightly occupation. Sailor Town was a warren of cheap bars, whore houses and decrepit living conditions. Sailor Town, like its companion, Soldier Town, was given that sobriquet because it was frequented by sailors out looking for pleasure. Alcohol, some drugs and mainly women. The Women's Christian Temperance Union was fighting a mighty battle for prohibition, but it was still a losing battle in 1916.

Halifax had always been a port city, but the influx of sailors during the war created a demand for their raging hungers that could only be satiated in a place like Sailor Town. A lonely sailor, drunk and looking for sex, all too often said things that could land them in dire circumstance if their superior officers ever found out about it.

Not only was Sailor Town a haven for prostitutes, its many bars and illicit liquor establishments catered to all the lowlife Halifax had on tap. It was the right place for conspiracies to be discussed. And sometimes overheard.

For some reason, Harry had taken a liking to Packy. Although he inhabited the sleazier parts of civilization, Packy had a heart of gold. In the same way that prostitutes did, or so romantics claimed. It was useful to have someone like Packy around. He had access to information that was unavailable to most law-abiding citizens. And you never know, maybe by chance he might unearth a German spy.

17

25 June 1916. Halifax.

THE PILOT HOUSE WAS LOCATED ON THE SOUTH SLOPE OF Citadel Hill, down in the bowels of a shanty neighbourhood. Ben was thinking it sure was a fancy name for such a shitty drinking place. The main floor offered some restaurant fare, if you liked greasy Chinese food. Rumour had it that there were back rooms where you could have a pipe of opium. Out of sight and out of mind.

He entered a dark hallway that had been tunneled into the side of the hill. Down a few steps there was another drinking space. A very private place with few patrons. Although Ben sometimes met Danny at the Pig, he didn't like to be seen there with him very often. This place was better.

It was only 4:30 on Wednesday afternoon, but Danny had a half-downed whiskey next to a dented tankard of Oland's finest.

"Starting early, are you Danny?"

"Nope. Just preparing myself for our meeting. Like saying grace before a meal." Danny was sporting a mean looking bruise stretching back from his left eyebrow.

"Huh! Sometimes I wonder about you, Danny. Sometimes you just don't seem like you have the loyalty needed for this line of work. Be assured, I'm not a fool and I will not tolerate fools around me. A lot of people think that war is a great romantic adventure, and if that's all you are here for, we might as well part company now."

"Hold your horses, Ben, for God's sake. I'm Irish, not German. England is probably more of an enemy to me than it is to you. That's why my sympathies lie with Germany's struggle. And it's why it pisses me off that Americans are helping to supply Germany's enemies, especially the British, with vital supplies." Danny considered himself a gun for hire. While he wanted to take out his contempt on all Americans for helping the enemy, he wanted to do it on his own terms. At least, he did not want to be dictated to by this German.

Ben had heard this argument before. It was a good argument but he still nursed a nagging suspicion about Danny's commitment. "I know. I know this, Danny. But I still need a reliable partner more than I need your impassioned anger. Deeds are the currency I count on."

"Relax, Ben. I'm not a hot-head like you are sometimes. I move at a slower pace. You might take a lesson from the turtle and the hare. I may not run as fast as you do, but I'm heading in the same direction. Trust me."

Ben grunted. He still had a nagging feeling about Danny. It was like Danny was in in the army but he didn't quite salute properly. *Not a crisp military salute like me*, he thought. "Danny, we have a job coming up. I don't know all the details, but there's a ship arriving in Halifax that is of particular concern to our friends in New York. It will arrive in about three weeks and will be in port for three or four days before joining a convoy to England."

"So, some more work in the service of the Kaiser!"

"Easy, Danny. I know we are alone, but you have to watch your language. That's part of the reason I worry about you. You don't have enough sense of secrecy. You have to pretend that people will eavesdrop on your conversation if what you say is interesting to them, especially if it has to do with war news."

"Yes, sir!"

"In the meantime, we need to prepare for a rendezvous off the coast, somewhere south of Lunenburg. There are lots of little bays and coves along that stretch of coastline, and they're often used by rum runners. Some of the locals know what about this. A little bit of cash offered to the right fisherman can oftentimes persuade that person to take his boat out for some night fishing."

"Why would they deal with us? Rum is one thing but…"

"Keep your voice down, Danny. God damn it," Ben whispered." We are going to be rum runners. As long as our man thinks that and he gets paid, he'll be thinking of booze and not bombs."

"I'm assuming you have a plan for all this?"

"I ain't whistling Dixie, my Irish friend. Of course, I've got a plan. As a matter of fact, you and I are taking a little drive down along the coast this Sunday morning. We're going to see a man about a boat. On that drive I'll give you all the details about our upcoming mission."

18

9 November 1917. New York.

"IT IS A MAGNIFICENT CITY, DON'T YOU THINK, JEAN?"

Jean Glotin was the first officer aboard the *Mont Blanc*. Although Aimé Le Médec was the captain, his English was very sparse, something he was ashamed of. He didn't understand the mechanics of the language. He was very self-conscious every time he had to deal with American authorities in his capacity as Captain of the *Mont Blanc*. Glotin, on the other hand, was quite fluent in the language.

Le Médec liked Glotin and trusted him, but he chafed at the necessity of relying on him to represent their interests whenever English was the language of the situation.

"Yes, Aimé, I quite agree. Maybe it lacks the refinement of Paris, but it truly is one of the world's great cities. What it lacks in a long pedigree it more than makes up for in excitement. A bustling city with a fabulous future to look forward to."

Early on this bright fall day, with leaves still clinging to many trees, the *Mont Blanc* arrived at the approaches to New York.

Their pilot, Randy Smith, came aboard just as they arrived at a spot with a clear view of the West Bank lighthouse. He had new orders for the captain. Randy had a vague feeling of guilt, as if he were delivering a death notice from the Admiralty: *Your son died bravely in battle.* Randy knew what cargoes were loaded in Gravesend Bay. He handed over the papers.

"These orders are from Edward Flower, who, as you know, is the New York agent for the French Government. I am to pilot this ship to Gravesend Bay in Brooklyn, where you will be docked for the duration of your stay."

"But this is not our usual berth," protested Le Médec. He was very upset. "Jean, please ask him why are we being diverted. I have a bad feeling that Edward Flower has been keeping information from us."

It was Edward Flower's job to commission the ships and arrange the cargoes and transportation from New York back to France. He had a job to do, and it was up to him how that that job got done. Whatever he needed to do, it would be arranged to meet the demands of the French Government. If that meant being a bit disingenuous with Captain Le Médec regarding their cargo then so be it!

Le Médec's suspicions only grew worse when the pilot handed him plans from the Board of Underwriters to line every inch of the holds of the *Mont Blanc* with wood and to use only copper nails in the construction. He knew that copper nails were only used to prevent an accidental ignition of flammable cargo, because they did not spark when struck. Dire thoughts fluttered through Le Médec's mind, leaving a wake of dread to add to his growing unease with the unfolding mission. He wondered if he would ever see his family again.

19

27 June 1916. Halifax.

PACKY'S FAVOURITE TAVERN, THE PIG'S REVENGE, WAS located on Upper Water Street. Like all other taverns, it was a men-only drinking establishment. Unlike a lot of the other drinking holes that catered to anyone, this place was clean and had little alcoves where you could drink with your friends and enjoy a bit of privacy. It also offered good pub food. For two dollars, you could get a hot chicken sandwich with peas and French fries and lots of gravy. With a few skinny glasses of tap beer for five cents apiece.

If you wanted something fancier, maybe for a nice girl you were dating, you could go up to Spring Garden Road and find a table for two at the Lord Nelson Hotel. On the other hand, if you were a student or you wanted to go slumming for an easy lay, there were many dives down in Sailor Town. But the Pig's Revenge was the favourite place to meet your male friends for something to eat and many drinks to last you into the wee hours.

Harry Frobisher was wearing a light summer suit when he pushed through the front door of the Pig on this beautiful June day. *I should be taking the day off,* he thought with some sense of loss. *Days like this just don't happen very often at this time of year. Liz and I could be sitting in Point Pleasant Park right now, or going somewhere nice for a picnic Maybe drive down to Hubbards, although it would still be kind of chilly for that.*

"Isn't it a little early for you to be at the tavern, Harry?" Billy had been the bartender at the Pig's Revenge for as long as Harry could remember. *I am sure he served my father when he was a young man*, Harry thought.

"Well Billy, I could be here for lunch, you know. I could be drinking coffee. Maybe if it was Saturday, I'd have a drink, but not on a working day."

"So, you are working right now, are you Harry?"

"As a matter of fact, I am. I want to enlist your help. Borrow your ears."

"I'm your man, Harry."

"I'm interested in a couple of fellers. They might be your customers. One guy is tall and thin, very erect. Bit of an intimidating presence. Could be a military man by the way he carries himself. The other guy is shorter, with a big pile of curly red hair, balding a bit. I don't know if they are regulars or not, but they might have been in here last Friday. Maybe they work on the docks. Might come in here after work."

"What am I looking for Harry?"

"I'd say probably the one with curly red hair and a short stature. If he's with someone else the other person would be the military looking man and would probably look like he was in good shape. You wouldn't mistake them for business men."

"What should I do, Harry? Call you and say I saw someone suspicious lurking in a dark corner of the pub?"

"Don't take the Mick out on me, Billy. We're friends, right? Just keep your eyes peeled and your ear to the ground. You can do that without making anyone feel like they are being spied on. Maybe you'll hear a casual remark. Something will catch your attention. You'll know. All I'm trying to do is to form a picture of these two. And Billy, it has to be on the QT. Just between us."

Harry was not a person prone to believe in conspiracies or to accept things on faith. His wife kept telling him not to question Catholic doctrine so much, or it would destroy his faith. "But dear, I can't help being like Sherlock Holmes. I have a mind and a rational brain, and that is how I live. I need evidence and I need to examine whatever facts are available, be it religious doctrine or a criminal investigation. It's how I should solve crimes. Logic serves me better than faith in the pursuit of truth. A suspicion, like this one proffered by Packy, will probably turn out to be a pipe dream but, who knows. We'll see. If I think there is evidence to be found I will follow the trail."

"As a matter of fact," Billy exclaimed, "I just may have a tidbit for you. Nothing suspicious regarding spies or secret agents, but there was a guy here a couple of days ago with red hair. I mean curly red hair that stands out."

"And?"

"I might've even seen him before, but my mind is kind of fuzzy on that. He was in here in the early evening. Sat at that table right next to the bar. He was by himself. Told me he was celebrating his birthday. Wanted some Jameson Irish Whiskey. He was very upset when I told him we only had Bushmills.

"So, Irish?"

"As Irish as they come. Big round head. A face full of freckles. Receding hairline. Dirty blue eyes. Suspicious eyes, I'd say. Sneered at my offer of Bushmills. Called it Protestant crap."

"Did he have an accent, Billy?"

"No. Not that you'd notice. Could've been born here or the accent could've worn away after so many years over here. It was the red hair, but more his surly attitude that triggered my recollection. One more thing, Harry. All that furor in Ireland back in April—what they call the Irish uprising?"

"Of course, I remember. Some guy named Pearse was the leader. Wanted to establish Ireland as a republic. Five days of fighting with hundreds killed."

"Right. When the redhead received his large glass of Bushmills, he toasted his own birthday. But he also toasted this guy Pearse. I didn't twig it at the time, but the more I read about those events in Ireland, it suddenly occurred to me that he was toasting the uprising ringleader, Patrick Pearse. Had to be."

"That's interesting, Billy. Doesn't seem like he's a big fan of the English. The Irish nationalists who are fighting to drive the British out of Ireland make no bones about who they support in the war between England and Germany. I wonder where his sympathies lie, our man with the red hair?"

"As you are aware, Harry, we're fortunate here in Halifax that Catholics and Protestants live quite happily side by side. You rarely see the kind of animosity that that chap showed the other day."

"I appreciate your help, Billy. As Confucius says, a journey of a thousand miles starts with a single step. Let me know if you see this guy in here again. Especially if he's accompanied by a military-looking gentleman. Take care."

20

16 July 1916. Off the coast of Lunenburg.

"I SEE IT." IT WAS A LITTLE PAST 2 AM. BEN AND DANNY were huddled in the Cape Islander with their nervous captain. The boat was tied to a rusted rail on the remains of an old decaying dock. "Just where you said it would be. Out there on that rough water. Two flashes and then three more. "That's the signal," said Danny.

A few weeks back, over a couple of weekends, Ben had sniffed around places like Lunenburg and Mahone Bay looking for a boat for hire. He'd let it be known that he had some work for the right person with their own boat. People knew not to ask why, only to whisper his request to specific people who were interested in making some unrecorded money.

The captain's name was Cyril Tobias. Everyone called him Toby. He lived by himself in a weather-beaten old wooden house out near Blue Rocks. His wife had died a long time ago. His only companion was an orange tabby cat, a good mouser who liked nothing better than to display his prizes on the front stoop. Toby owned a Cape Islander that he kept in good shape. His weather-beaten face attested to a life on the sea and more rum than was healthy for an old coot like him.

To most people around the Lunenburg area, he was harmless. Just a friendly soul who didn't bother anyone. He fished for a living, but no one could figure out how he could survive on the meagre catches he sold to the local fish market. Some rumours suggested that he was a rum runner. Nothing big time, just an occasional trip. And only if the money was right and he trusted the contact. Which is how he had made the acquaintance of Ben and his red-haired accomplice.

*   *   *

Back at the beginning of May, shortly after Ben had had his demonstration of the cigar bombs in New Jersey, Koeing had met with him one last time and assured Ben that he had been approved for a trial run as a test of Ben's abilities. Ben would be supplied with two crates of cigar bombs, to be delivered by freighter to a rendezvous off the Nova Scotia coast.

At the beginning of July he had received a telegram from Koeing suggesting he meet with a Mr. Smith, a businessman from New York who had business in Halifax. The meeting had taken place in the departure lounge of the railway station in the Nova Scotian Hotel last Tuesday, on the day Mr. Smith was to board his train for the return trip to New York.

At that Tuesday meeting Mr. Smith had advised Ben that Koeing had received some interesting information from his agent who worked at National City Bank in New York. The agent had come across a telegram from the London Procurement Office with several purchase orders for war supplies. This telegram also included a list of the ships carrying these cargos, along with their arrival and departure dates. One of these ships would be leaving in a convoy from Halifax near the end of July.

In addition to giving Ben the intelligence about the ship, Smith had also given him precise instructions for a rendezvous with a freighter off the coast of Nova Scotia. He would need a reliable boat, along with a trustworthy captain. And Smith had given him $500 in cash. "That's a token gesture from our mutual friend to be used as payment for your hired boat."

* * *

It was bitterly cold as they rode the boat out to freighter. A low fog smelling foully of salty air curled around them as they approached their target. The fog reminded Ben of an old cat that was suspicious of everything that came near it and wanted to make sure there was no danger to itself lurking nearby.

They unloaded the crates and stowed them under some nets and canvas tarps. The journey back to the cove was uneventful, given that they were shrouded completely by the fog. They unloaded their cargo near the abandoned old rusty wharf and carried it into the long grass to a lean-to that Ben and Danny had prepared beforehand. There was an old pitted dirt road that ran near the lean-to but it was never used. The cargo was safe from detection. They had stowed the four crates and covered them with the tarp and some old rotting lumber that had been part of the collapsed structure.

Toby had done a good job in pulling alongside the freighter. His nervousness had not hampered his ability. Ben guessed that it was shoved way to the back of his mind by the promise of $500. And to further convince Toby that they were rum runners, in case he was in any way suspicious, Ben had secretly hidden a case of rum in the long grass, which he presented to Toby after the cargo was unloaded.

21

25 July 1916. Halifax.

"EVENING, HARRY. WOULD YOU BE WANTING A LITTLE tickle before you head home to the little woman?" It was after five on a Tuesday evening, on a very hot and sweaty day. There was not a stir of a breeze from the harbour when Harry arrived at the Pig's Revenge. He had his suit jacket over his left shoulder. The jacket was hooked in place by his right thumb, revealing a wet patch under his armpit.

"If Liz heard you refer to her as the little woman, she would have to go straight to confession for uttering swear words. She strongly believes in the women's suffrage movement. And, as a matter of fact, so do I."

"Sorry, Harry. I didn't mean any offence. It was just a harmless greeting. You do hear it in here all the time."

"The thing is, Billy, it is never bandied about in polite society. But I'm not here to talk about trivial conversation. I'm here in response to the message you left me at the station house."

"If you won't have a beer, how about some coffee? I made a pot less than ten minutes ago. And I've got some fresh cream as well. How about it?"

"I'll take it. They say a hot drink is supposed to be good on a hot day."

"Coming right up, Harry. Have a seat at the bar. I'll be right with you."

"You mentioned in your note that you saw our Irish friend."

"Last Friday. We often get a bunch of guys in here after work. Stevedores who work on the docks. They come in here when their shifts end, usually around 4:30. And last Friday was a hot one, just like today. They didn't come in for coffee though." Billy smiled. "This group included the curly red-headed guy. I gathered he was a newcomer with this crew. Most of the others were regulars I recognized, including one guy who fit the description you gave me before."

"You mean the military-looking guy? The one Packy said he saw with the Irishman a few months ago?"

"That's the guy. He doesn't come in here all that often, but when he does it's with his group of fellow workers. Not the friendliest bloke in town. Tall, thin guy. Hatchet face. Menacing eyes. Steel grey hair, severely cut like he was in the service. Acts more like the one in charge rather than one of the guys, if you get my meaning. If it were a military group, he'd be the captain and the others would be under his command. They're friendly to him but deferential."

"And Red, how did he fit in?"

"A little aloof. Mostly he talked to the military guy—the one someone in the group addressed as Ben. It was busy and I didn't have much of chance to listen to their conversations. I think they were mainly talking about getting laid that night."

"Now that doesn't surprise me, Billy. Friday night. Payday. Your first appetite is being addressed at the bar. It's your second appetite that needs to be attended to." Harry finished off the last dregs of his coffee and set his cup back on the bar. He was itching to get home and change out of his limp suit.

"Thank you for the coffee, Billy. And I really do appreciate your observations. Did they stay long?"

"Naw. The group stayed for a while, but Ben and Red left after two rounds. I can't say they left together, but they both left at about the same time."

After he left the Pig for the short drive home in his two-year-old Ford, Harry wondered if there was any connection between this Ben fellow and the Irishman.

22

30 July 1916. New Jersey.

IF YOU WERE STANDING IN BATTERY PARK AT THE SOUTH-
ern end of Manhattan Island, looking across the Hudson towards
New Jersey, you would see the Statue of Liberty welcoming visitors and new immigrants to America. And if you looked past the
statue, and a bit closer at the Jersey shore line, you would also
notice a mile-long spit of land jutting out into the harbour. That
spit of land looked, at least from some angles, like a black tomcat
arched up on its hind legs. That was Black Tom.

Housing over two million tons of war materials, Black Tom was
the largest ammunition depot in the United States. Even though
there was no declared war between America and Germany, these
military supplies were transparently destined for shipment to the
Allies fighting in Europe.

Early on this Sunday morning, most of this ammunition,
which was packed in train cars in the Black Tom railroad yards,
exploded. The detonation was fierce, sending bullets and shells
flying into the night sky. It rocked the harbour, sending nearby
residents tumbling from their beds. The explosion was heard as
far away as Maryland and Connecticut. The Statue of Liberty was
severely damaged by flying shrapnel.

The immediate investigation into the explosion focused on two
night watchmen who had lit smudge pots to keep mosquitos at

bay. They were questioned by police, but after an extensive interrogation they were released without further suspicion. The police had no other suspects and determined that the explosion was an unfortunate accident. Even President Wilson remarked that it was a regrettable incident at a private railroad terminal.

The investigation was handed over to the Interstate Commerce Commission. Their investigation eventually determined that this was not an accident but an act of sabotage orchestrated by agents of the German government. The intent was to destroy ammunition destined for the Allies.

Suspicion soon fell upon the German Naval intelligence officer, Franz von Rintelen. He had the resources, and he was also linked to a suspicious pharmacist in Hoboken, Dr. Walter Scheele, who was suspected of espionage. At this time the United States did not have an established national intelligence service. There was not even a federal statute forbidding peacetime espionage or sabotage. Security communications between various investigative departments was rudimentary, and made connections to the saboteurs and their accomplices impossible to track.

Life on the New York waterfront continued much as usual, although public opinion started to shift against Germany in the aftermath of the explosion. The ongoing reports of ships exploding at sea after leaving New York continued to feed suspicions of an ongoing sabotage campaign against the neutral United States.

23

15 August 1916. Halifax.

THE S.S. *WILLIAM SEVERANCE* WAS A 447-FOOT STEEL hull cargo ship with 8,286 gross tonnage. Her home port was Liverpool, England, and she carried a crew of eleven men. She arrived in Halifax on 10 August from New York with a partial cargo of lumber and machinery parts that were badly needed for England's dwindling supply of industrial goods. Her forward cargo bay was empty and was to be filled with medical supplies in Halifax.

Normally, she would have been berthed in Bedford Basin, but she had been directed to dock at Pier 8 since her arrival last Thursday afternoon, the 10th of August. She was waiting to complete her final loading on Monday before leaving in a convoy on Wednesday the 15th. Her security in port consisted of a single watchman for daytime and another for the night shift. Even though it was wartime, Halifax was not on a war footing, and a general calm pervaded the port city. There was no special concern about German saboteurs.

At this stage of the war, many local men had left to volunteer with the British forces fighting on the continent. Conscription had not yet been adopted. The Canadian Prime Minister, Robert Bordon, had vowed that no Canadian would be sent to war unless he volunteered. Something like one in three had volunteered, and as a consequence there was a general shortage of labour.

It didn't take long for available workers to be scooped up by a hungry labour market, where demand always seemed to be higher than supply. That was also part of the reason Danny Sullivan, with a little help from Ben Stendt, had no trouble finding work on the waterfront.

Ben had worked on the waterfront for twelve years, and was a familiar figure on the dockyards. People might have wondered why, at 34, he wasn't a volunteer in the Canadian army, but his tall stature and piercing grey eyes were intimidating enough for most people to refrain from approaching that subject. His reluctance to discuss anything about his personal life put a quick end to any questioning along those lines.

Although Ben wasn't the friendliest person in the world, he wasn't afraid of hard work, and his bosses respected that. He was often chosen as a shift foreman because he was a natural leader. His assignment today was to supervise the loading of the S.S. *William Severance*. Ben had been successful at including Danny in the work detail, even though Danny was a relative newcomer to the ranks of stevedores working on the waterfront.

Ben had, on at least one occasion, stood up for one of his fellow workers when that man had been accused of assaulting a seaman from a visiting merchant ship. As the ship was being loaded, a strap broke on a pallet being raised by the ship's crane, spilling a load of grain sacks. One of the sacks hit a crew member on the shoulder, knocking him down. He wasn't injured, but he sounded off against the stevedore operating the crane and grabbed him roughly by his coat sleeve.

The ship's first mate complained to the authorities, accusing the stevedore of negligence and assaulting his crewman. Ben had been present during the incident, and he strongly defended the stevedore and convinced the authorities the stevedore was justified in throwing a punch at the seaman. He said he would have done the same thing. The authorities let it go, and Ben's stock rose in the minds of his fellow stevedores.

Security for the waterfront included official pass cards, but in reality was based more on familiarity than anything else. Ben's arm over Danny's shoulder, cursory as it was, reduced any suspicions that the checkpoint guard might have. The S.S. *William Severance* was not deemed a high-risk situation. It was freighter loading a non-military cargo. No one suspected that six "cigar" bombs had been secreted into the cargo hold.

The cargo of medical supplies was fully loaded without incident by early afternoon on Monday, and the S.S. *William Severance* was moved to the Basin. She was assigned a spot in the convoy among nineteen other vessels, and the entire brace of ships set sail just before sunrise on Wednesday morning.

On Saturday, 19 August, a telegraph report reached Halifax about the mysterious explosion aboard the S.S. *William Severance.* There had been no reported sightings of German U-boats in the area, and the seas were calm for the most part, except for some choppy water around the time of the explosion. The four days that the convoy had been at sea after leaving Halifax had been uneventful up until that time.

It had been just after the evening meal when the explosion occurred. Witnesses said they were still cleaning dishes when there was a loud bang. At first, they thought that they had been torpedoed but that was soon ruled out. Captain Simone Le Metis had no explanation for the explosion. He said it just went *boom!*

Reports told of a jagged hole in the forward hold on the port side of the ship. It was below the water line, and attempts to stem the breach proved futile. The ship began to list to port and the captain gave the order to abandon ship at around twenty-two hundred hours. All hands survived and were safely rescued by two shadowing ships. The S.S. *William Severance* sank below the waves at zero two-hundred hours.

There had been reports over the past year about mysterious explosions aboard ships leaving in convoy out of New York, but this was the first time something like this had happened to a convoy out of Halifax.

24

16 Nov 1917. New York.

THE SUN HAD SET BY THE TIME AIMÉ HAD JOINED Alphonse and Jean in the booth of a small restaurant serving working class men. There were a few women, but mostly it was men who made their livelihood working on the waterfront. The restaurant, Barney's, served staples like hamburgers, hot dogs and open-faced sandwiches. And Barney would make you breakfast any time of the day. And coffee. Lots and lots of coffee. Also, by request only, you could get a dram of rum in your coffee from a hidden bar.

There were few customers when the three men sat down in the early evening. It was quiet and private, which was why they were here now. They would be speaking French, so they weren't worried about strangers eavesdropping on their conversation.

Barney's wife, who did most of the cooking, had already left for the day, leaving Barney and two other staff to look after stragglers until closing time at eight.

Alphonse and Jean were already drinking spiked coffee when Aimé squeezed into the booth.

Jean signaled Barney, "Another of your fine coffees, please, for our fine captain." As the presumed spokesman when English was used, Jean took his cue automatically.

"Gentlemen, it has been a hectic week. I am glad of this little interlude and the chance to discuss what we have accomplished so far and what remains to be done."

Alphonse took a deep draw on his pipe and Aimé warned him, "You won't be able to do that on our open deck when the cargo is fully loaded, my dear friend. Way too dangerous."

Aimé, do we have a complete list of the ammunition we will be carrying?"

"The first of the cargo arrives on Wednesday, along with our agent, Edward Flower, who has promised to bring a copy of the complete manifest with him. We will find out then what that sneaky little man has been hiding from us." Aimé said this with some bitterness in his voice. "I know he is sneaky. He told us there would be some ammunition. He didn't tell us the whole boat would become a floating ammunitions storage magazine."

Jean summarized what the crew had accomplished over the last eleven days. "The plans we had from the Board of Underwriters were very clear and specific. It's a good thing that among our crew of 39 men we had so many skilled in carpentry. And so many other able-bodied men to help with the work. Every single square inch of the hold has been lined with wood. There are no metal surfaces that can be seen."

Alphonse took another greedy draw on his pipe. "Some of the men were griping about wearing those cloth slippers over their boots. Said they made their boots slippery. I told them it was to protect the cargo from sparks when it was being loaded. They weren't too happy with that information."

"Nonetheless, they did an excellent job." Jean continued. "All those cribs they made and those dividers. It was a lot of work. So, I say, good for them. They are a fine crew."

Aimé took a sip of his coffee. "What about the ammunition for our two guns?" The *Mont Blanc* had two 90-millemetre guns, one fore and the other aft. Before they arrived in New York the gun crew had fired off some practice rounds, but over three hundred live shells remained, some on deck and the rest in lower compartments. "Those all need to be stored on deck in case we need them, God forbid."

Jean responded, "All taken care of. The Board made sure of that in their detailed plans."

Aimé was well aware that the crew were getting restless. He could also sense their growing dread about this voyage. He had been brought up a Catholic, but his years at sea, away from any regular churchgoing, had dulled whatever faith clung to him from his youth. Praying was something you did in church, or on other momentous occasions. He did it by rote and didn't put much store in it. But the growing risk of this voyage was causing him to revalue his feelings of getting help wherever he could get it.

"What do you think, Jean?" he asked in a weary voice. "How long before we will be able to leave New York for Nova Scotia?"

"I know, Aimé, that everyone is getting anxious to get this voyage over with. Including the three of us. My best guess is that we will be here until the end of the month. They are going to start loading in two days. They are still waiting for a shipment that won't arrive until the weekend. So, a week to ten days."

Aimé concluded, "Okay my good friends, let's get some rest and finish what we need to do tomorrow. We need to be fresh and ready for the loading on Wednesday."

25

21 August 1916. Halifax.

"THERE ARE A COUPLE OF COPPERS WAITING TO SPEAK TO you, Mr. Sullivan."

Danny Sullivan had been in a fight on Saturday night and had been knocked over the head with a two by four. The blow had been severe enough to put him into a coma from which he had not surfaced until late Sunday evening. He remembered drinking over at that cheap bar up on Gottingen Street. The Green Lantern. A lot of rummies held court there. And a lot of young coloured kids with chips on their shoulders, up from Africville.

The rummies were like rummies you would find in every cheap bar in the country. Both male and female. It didn't make a difference. They knew best how to win the war. If only the government did things the way these losers thought they should, then the war would be over before you knew it. Sage wisdom from low-lifes who would spit in their glass of beer so no one would drink it when they went for a piss. Argue with any of them at your peril. Which is what Danny did.

He had drunk too many quarts of that very fine Oland's beer. He knew he shouldn't have, and he also knew Ben would be so pissed off if he found out that Danny had yapped his mouth off about the goddamn Americans and their support for England.

"The Americans act like they are at war against Germany, but there's no declared war."

Danny remembered getting into a shoving match with a couple of big guys and taking a swing at one of them. He remembered being outside and on top of one of them, seeing the raised piece of lumber just before it knocked him out.

"Good morning, Mr. Sullivan. My name is Detective Harry Frobisher. I got your name and address from the admitting desk. First of all, I would like to confirm that information."

"What did they tell you?"

Harry spoke with a poker face. "They said your name is Danny Sullivan and you live in a boarding house over on Brunswick Street. And that you work as a stevedore up in the shipyards. That correct?"

"Yeah."

"They told me the only identification you had was a baptismal certificate."

"That's all I got. No passport."

"That baptismal certificate indicates you were baptized in Dublin, Ireland. I would've thought that Sullivan was more of a Scottish name than an Irish name."

"Let me give you officers a bit of education. There is an ancient clan in Ireland from down around County Cork called O'Suilleabhain. That's a Gaelic word. Over the years it got whittled down to O'Sullivan. And then people starting using just Sullivan, especially those who immigrated to America where Irish people were not always welcome. Can you imagine what it was like looking for employment and the sign on the front door says *Irish need not apply?*"

Harry could see the resentment in Danny's eyes. "I've heard those stories, but mainly they originated from New York and

Boston, where there are large Irish populations. But nothing like that in Canada. Tell me Danny, if you don't mind me calling you Danny, how long have you lived in Canada?"

"A couple of years," lied Danny. "I lived in New York for a while. Jobs weren't always easy to come by. I had heard good things about Halifax, so I decided to try my luck here."

"It seems you have done all right. Working as a stevedore is not a bad way to earn a living as long as you have the stamina and keep yourself fit. Do you have a name, maybe your boss, who could vouch for you?"

"You could always speak to the foreman. His name is Frank Simmons. But don't you go giving him any impression that I'm in trouble with the law. I don't want to lose my job."

"We won't do that," said Harry. "We would like to ask you a few questions about the other night. Tell me what you were arguing about that led to a fight."

"I don't remember a lot. Just that some bastard hit me over the head and knocked me out. Fucker hit me from behind."

"He surely did. By the time the police arrived you were out cold. Didn't come to until the next afternoon, Sunday. Can you tell us what happened?"

"I'll tell you what happened. Bunch of fuckin' Americans jumped me. We were having a somewhat heated discussion about the war. All of a sudden, this one guy jumps up and spills my beer onto my lap. Think I'm going to take that?"

"What were you arguing about?" Harry asked matter-of-factly.

"Do you know what, officer, I was born in Ireland. We have no great love for England, and I am sure that does not surprise you."

"Yes, I am quite aware of that, Danny."

"And we don't have any great love for Germany, either. So let the two countries fight it out. The thing that really rattles my chain is the fucking Americans. They are not at war with Germany or any other country that I'm aware of. So why're they acting like they are at war with Germany by supplying ammunition to England?"

"So, you got into a fight with a bunch of American seamen about it?"

"I guess that's the case, officer. There were three of them and they ambushed me. Are you going to do anything about it?"

"Alas, Danny, that is not possible, even if we wanted to. You were in a coma and we could find no other witnesses to speak to. Now it's Monday morning and all I can tell you is they probably shipped out on this morning's convoy to France. We don't even have their names."

"Fucking great! I guess that's it then."

Harry had his suspicions about this Irishman. He had a nagging doubt about Danny's residency in Halifax. Was this the guy that Packy was so suspicious of? "We just have to verify a few things about your employment and your boarding house. Routine stuff, you know? Then you're free to go."

26

24 August 1916. Halifax.

THE WEATHER COULD NOT HAVE BETTER. THERE WAS not a cloud to be seen anywhere in the bright blue sky. The high temperature was predicted to be 78 degrees Fahrenheit, and a modest breeze felt like a soothing cool caress from a pasha's ostrich feather. Harry wore his light tan suit, with a nice blue tie that looked stunning on the white background of his starched shirt. His father had been a military man, and a lot of his father's fastidiousness about being properly dressed found a home with the son.

Mid-morning found Harry and Sandy sitting in front of the chief of police. Mike Gallagher was a no-nonsense person who might have ruled with a firm hand, but he had no enemies on the Halifax police force. He treated everyone on the force with the same respect and expected everyone to follow his lead. He had the kind of respect any leader would give their eye teeth for.

Part of that respect was groomed by a willingness to listen to criticism of how he issued orders and directed police activities. The inference always was: I expect you to follow orders, but if you want to challenge me, I am ready to listen, as long as you are not frivolous in your feedback. I will not tolerate whiners.

"I want you two to head up a little task force. Maybe I shouldn't call it a task force yet, but I do want you to gather information for a project I have in mind. Depending on what information we can document, then maybe we can decide if we can make a plan of action. Harry, I want you and Sandy to take on this job. At the same time, I don't want this project to take away from your regular duties."

"Mike, I couldn't think of a person I would rather work with than Harry."

With an encouraging slap on Sandy's shoulder Harry replied, "Same goes for me, Captain."

Mike was very serious when he said, "There is always a danger in any investigation. I've seen this happen here in Halifax, and I've read about it happening countless times in all parts of the world. Someone gets an idea in his head. He thinks so-and-so is guilty and he goes looking for facts to back up that belief. And before you know it the whole damn department is in on the plot."

Sandy stroked his chin and said, "If we're suspicious about someone, isn't it natural to go looking for confirmation that they're guilty?"

"Indeed, it is, Sandy. Quite right. But what I am talking about is believing someone is guilty based on circumstantial evidence and then going out to find the facts to back up your belief. You lose your objectivity for examining facts on their own merit, and you don't care to look for evidence that points anywhere other than your obsessive objective. Circumstantial evidence is a great motivator, but it doesn't prove anything."

This kind of thinking was right up Harry's alley. Not only in police investigations but in everyday life, including his religious beliefs (much to the chagrin of his wife and especially Liz's family). "Well said, Mike. I absolutely agree with you. What do you have in mind for your stalwart investigators? We are ready."

Rolling his stiff neck around his shoulders, Mike started to summarize his thoughts. "Well, to start with, there's that British ship, the S.S. *William Severance*. Exploded four days after leaving Halifax harbour. No U-boats sighted. Just a mysterious explosion.

"Could it have been a bomb, maybe planted aboard her in Halifax? Who's to say, but it's one of those nagging thoughts that keeps my brain itchy. Harry, would you poke around a little up at the dockyard? Nothing obtrusive, just gather a bit of information about her time here in port. Anyone asks, just say you are gathering information for the ship's insurance company."

Harry nodded and said, "I agree with you wholeheartedly, Mike. That's definitely something to explore, even though we have no evidence to work with for now."

"Also," said Mike, "There was that massive explosion in New Jersey last month. The Black Tom ammo dump. At first, they thought it was an accident, but now they are investigating it as an act of sabotage orchestrated by German agents. They're also linking this explosion to all the mysterious explosions of ships leaving American shores over the past year or so. It's that kind of thinking that draws my attention to the S.S. *William Severance*."

Sandy agreed. "Well, we can't take our thoughts to the newspaper, but Harry and I will do what we can to see if we can make a meal out of this."

"Indeed," chimed in Harry.

27

31 August 1916. Halifax.

BEN WASN'T SURE ABOUT HIS ACCOMPLICE, DANNY Sullivan. *He's a tough guy, no doubt,* thought Ben, *but he drinks too much and he is careless with his mouth. Koeing told me to keep an eye on him, that he needed leadership. Does that mean I have to babysit him every goddamn hour of the day? He spends all his time with those floosies over in Sailor town and I really don't trust him not to whisper things to any of them when he drinks too much. Which is often.*

"Danny, we have to get ready for another 'placement.' There's a coal carrier that has been scheduled to leave on a convoy early next week. She's in the dry dock right now for repairs, but she has to take on a cargo of coal for the trip across the Atlantic. More vital war supplies for England."

They were sitting on a bench high up in Fort Needham, over-looking the dry dock and the panoramic view of the shipyards and the Narrows, where the harbour emptied into Bedford Basin. Looking south, they could see past the Old Town Clock and the posh South End, with its nose stuck up in the air as if it didn't agree with the smell of Sailor Town fowling the air in the center of the city.

Danny wore a rumpled white shirt with the sleeves rolled up to his elbows and a workman's cap. His baggy pants were held up with suspenders, and his nicotine-stained fingers nervously held a cigarette. As usual his bulging eyes looked like they were going to pop out from below his curly red hair. It was a nervous tic that was always triggered by stress. Like now. He was afraid of Ben.

"Are we going to wait until she moves over to the loading wharf?" asked Danny. They could easily see the target boat tied up to the dry dock. The S.S. *Port of Dover.*

"Not if we can get to her before she leaves the dry dock where she is getting repaired."

"How are we goanna be able to do that?" Danny was a little apprehensive.

"You and I are going to get aboard that ship this Sunday night. It's the Labour Day weekend, so anyone who can take the weekend off is going to do so. The only security will be a night watchman. They usually use old retired commissioners as night watchmen if there's no heightened security in effect. Since there is no cargo on board and the crew are ashore until Tuesday, Sunday night's our best bet."

"We still have to worry about the night watchman."

Ben was thinking about that. *Just kill him and dump him in the harbour.* Not that that would bother his conscience very much. If he even had a conscience these days. *For the Kaiser, then.* The main problem would be the discovery of the body. It would certainly draw attention to the ship if the watchman was killed while on duty.

"I suppose we could bribe him or threaten a family member," Ben offered, "but I don't see those as viable plans at all. We don't even know if he has a family member, and bribing the old geezer would probably backfire. Besides, we don't have much money for a bribe."

"What are we going to do then? Kill him?" Danny would have

no qualms about that, since he already had blood on his hands from Dublin.

Ben looked warily at Danny. "Yeah, I suppose so. But not unless we have to. I've another idea that might work. I'm going to try and distract him. If I act like I'm drunk and make my way up the gangplank as if I was one of the crew members wanting to claim his bunk, he might buy that. If I can distract him for ten minutes, you could easily climb down the ladder to the cargo hold and plant our cigar packages."

"Do you think he would buy that? Wouldn't he just tell you to get off of the ship?"

"That depends on his attitude. If he's a snarly old fart, he might just do that. However, if he's a friendly old guy, maybe no family, he just might be inclined to have a spot of rum to while away the night. I mean he's not guarding a fortune, just an empty old scow with nothing on it worth stealing. And if a crewman offers him a friendly drink, what could it hurt?"

28

3 September 1916. Halifax.

"I THOUGHT THAT WAS A FINE SERMON YOU GAVE THIS morning, Peter. Not too preachy on this holiday weekend. Just the right amount of uplifting spirit to go with the day." Harry said this with a straight face, but Peter was always suspicious he was being a little sarcastic.

"Thank you, Harry. I was thinking of you and what you once said to me: "Blessed are the brief of speech, for they shall be invited back again." Peter chuckled and thought to himself, *It doesn't hurt to show Harry that priests do have a sense of humour. It's not all serious business.*

There was still a slight bit of mist in the air, but the sun was gaining ground, and Harry was hopeful for a nice afternoon and maybe a stroll in the Public Gardens. Harry and Liz had driven her parents to St. Thomas Aquinas Church, where her brother Peter was celebrating the 10:00 AM mass.

"That's a saying I very much agree with," Harry said with a chuckle. There's one guy on the force that never stops yacking. I should invite you in to give him some of the same advice. And there are a couple of politicians I can think of that could also use your counselling. Does it matter if they are Catholics, or do you minister to other faiths, Peter?"

"Are you trying to bait me, Harry? It wouldn't be the first time."

Harry could see Liz giving him the evil eye. Even her mother had raised a menacing eyebrow. They were standing around by the back of the glebe house, getting ready for the drive back to Tower Road. Dinner would be served around noon. Harry wasn't a ranter, even though he had a lot of gripes about the power of the Catholic Church here in Halifax. He murmured to himself and flashed a friendly smile to Peter.

"You know what, Peter? It's the long weekend, and we should enjoy it together in a pleasant way. I shall not make another comment about religion, because it's not appropriate. And by the way, I really did like your sermon."

After their roast beef dinner, which Harry thought was a bit overcooked, they were chatting away in good cheer and finishing the remains of the wine when Donald asked Harry, "Does the police force ever get involved in investigating rumours of German saboteurs actively working underground in Halifax?"

"Interesting you should mention that, Donald. Just a week ago our captain, Mike Gallagher, who you know very well, asked us to begin a discreet investigation. There have always been rumours, especially about German agents about to blow up the submarine nets strung across the harbour. But we've never had any evidence to pursue an investigation."

Harry continued, "To the best of our knowledge no one has ever tried to blow up the submarine nets. It's a daily rumour that is fueled by a general fear that the Germans could attack us here in Halifax. The general population has a greater fear that the Germans will drop bombs on us."

"Those are the rumours I hear every day, Harry." Donald offered.

"I hear those rumours as well, Donald. They are not what triggered this investigation, though. We've started a discreet investigation based on some circumstantial evidence. First of all, there was the mysterious explosion of the S.S. *William Severance* a few days after leaving Halifax in a convoy bound for England. We believe a time bomb was secreted aboard that ship in Halifax long before she left our port.

"We've heard so many stories of ships leaving New York and exploding several days later, far out at sea. It's an accepted fact in the U.S. that there's an underground network of German saboteurs working in New York and New Jersey. And these agents are probably funded by the German government."

"And you think they're operating here in Halifax as well?" questioned Donald.

"We have no evidence, just the fact that the ship was in Halifax, took on some supplies here and later blew up at sea. Our question is, what if someone here planted a bomb? Our circumstantial evidence also gets a boost from all those American incidences. Add to that the Black Tom explosion in New York. You know, that ammunition dump that blew up in New Jersey at the end of July. It just adds to our suspicions, and that's why we began our investigation."

29

3 September 1916. Night. Halifax.

BEN AND DANNY HAD NO TROUBLE SLINKING THEIR WAY onto the dry dock where the SS *Port of Dover* was berthed. They both wore dark clothes and the night was completely overcast, with a light mist and rolling wisps of fog. They choose to arrive around 11:30 so that Ben's arrival on the deck of the boat would seem plausible to the night watchman. A drunken crew member sneaking on board after a night in Sailor Town, disobeying orders to remain in the boarding house where most of the crew were billeted.

The collier had been constructed with a two-story bridge in the center of the ship. Behind the bridge were crew quarters that could accommodate eight seamen. There were two coal storage holds, one forward and one aft. There was a single funnel at the stern. The empty forward hold was open, awaiting a replacement cover that was to be installed on Tuesday.

Ben crept up the slippery gangplank and made his way to the upper deck, where he crouched in the shadow of the bridge. The wet, salty air stung his nostrils as he waited to see if he had aroused the attention of the night watchman. The gangplank was below the bridge and quite visible if you were standing looking out the side window but not if you were sitting or dozing off. Danny waited on the wharf in a deep shadow.

"Who's there?" mumbled a hoarse old voice from the open door of the pilot's house on the upper deck."

He must have heard something, thought Ben. *No matter, I'll just have to fake it.* "Hold your horses, old man, I'm just going to my bunk," slurred Ben in his imitation of a drunk."

He lurched toward the crew quarters as the old man gripped the upper rail and yelled at Ben to leave. "You can't go back there. In fact, you shouldn't even be on board. Get out of here or I'll call the cops."

"Isokayyy. I just need something from my bunk. And I'll be gone." Ben staggered a bit and grabbed hold of the rail of the steps leading up to the pilot house.

While the watchman's attention was focused on Ben, Danny managed to climb up the gangplank and find the ladder going down into the empty hold. He climbed down to the bottom of the hold where the coal would be loaded on Tuesday. He had six cigar bombs, each with a six-day fuse that Ben had armed earlier in the day.

The sulfuric acid had already started to eat at the copper plugs. The fuses weren't entirely accurate and sometimes exploded prematurely. The bombs were timed to explode the following Saturday. *As long as they are well out to sea*, he thought. *Who cares if they explode early?*

Danny managed to hide them at the very front of the boat, three on either side. There were enough pieces of coal left over in the hold from the previous cargo to easily conceal the bombs without arousing any suspicion. A casual inspection of the hold would only reveal some remnants from the last cargo.

The night watchman is being such an arse, thought Ben. *If he is being so nosey and suspicious, he will probably sound an alarm as soon as I leave the boat. Can't have that.*

"All right, all right, I'm goin'," he slurred as he staggered for the old man's benefit.

"Damn right you're goin', you lousy drunk," whined the old man.

It didn't matter to Ben if Danny had made it safely back to the wharf or not; he was going to do what he had to do. Ben suddenly jerked around and bounded up the inside stairs. He roughly grabbed the old man by his shirt and flung him against the rail that overlooked the empty hold three stories below. The old man stumbled and lost his balance. He would have recovered from the stumble if Ben had not given him a shove. He tumbled over the railing and fell fifty feet to the steel hull, breaking his neck.

Danny was just starting his upward climb when all this happened. He went back down and examined the night watchman and he could easily see from the position of the body that a lot more bones were broken than just his neck. *Oh shit*, he said to himself, *this is more than I bargained for.*

Danny climbed up to the deck where Ben was waiting for him. "You fucking arsehole, you killed him. That wasn't part of the plan."

"Calm down, Danny or I'll throw you down alongside him. Let's just get the hell outta here. They won't discover him for hours until his shift is up. It looks like an accident; can't you see that? This boat is a coal carrier, and that means it has a low security designation. There is no motive for someone to murder the night watchman. The deck's slippery, he's an old man and tragically he fell while making his rounds."

The foggy night carried the muffled sound of a bell tolling in the distance. A reminder to weary souls of the lurking presence of the grim reaper.

30

4 September 1916. Halifax.

HARRY ARRIVED AT THE STATION HOUSE AT EXACTLY 7:00 AM on Monday morning. He was quite relaxed and well rested after a nice visit with his in-laws on Sunday, followed by a very pleasant stroll in Point Pleasant Park with Liz and Millie.

Dinner had been enjoyable and the conversation was light-hearted. Donald had been on his best behavior and had not ranted about the provincial government's incompetence, as he tended to do every Sunday. *Donald was probably scolded by his wife beforehand to zipper his lips about his opinions*, Harry thought. That was fine with Harry, who really didn't like these discussions, if you could call them discussions. Donald's rants didn't invite opposing points of view.

Harry had been sound asleep when he received a 5 AM phone call directly from Mike Gallagher, the Police Chief. "I'm so sorry to bother you at home Harry, especially on the Labour Day week-end, and I would not have done so if it could have waited."

"What's up Mike?" he said with an alarmed voice. Their phone was mounted on the wall next to the front hall closet. Liz had reached it before Harry had even opened his eyes. Liz had to go back up to the bedroom and give Harry a good shake before he understood that the chief of police was calling him. He grabbed his dressing gown and headed downstairs, all the while trying to smooth his hair, which was sticking straight up in places. The phone's ear piece was hanging down on its cord like a carpenter's plumb line.

"There's been an accident up at the dockyards, Harry. They found a night watchman dead at the bottom of a hold of a collier that was in for repairs. They're not saying that it's foul play, but they are a little suspicious. They want to move the body because the ship is being repaired and is scheduled to leave in a convoy on Wednesday. I've called Sandy and he will meet you in the office around seven. He'll have more details than I have."

"I'll be there, Mike. Duty is duty."

"Thanks, Harry. Again, sorry to ruin your holiday."

Harry was dressed in his brown summer suit, which was mainly his official uniform since being promoted to detective. He had other versions of this suit and a couple of blue ones that were reserved for special occasions. Thanks to Liz, his shirts were always crispy white to go with his selection of bow ties that Liz, for the most part, had carefully chosen for him. His suits were roomy enough to pretty well conceal his under-arm revolver.

"Well, Harry, how're you enjoying the holiday so far"? Sandy said with a welcoming grin. "At least I hope you and Liz and Millie had an enjoyable Sunday."

"As a matter of fact, Sandy, it was a great Sunday. We had dinner at the in-laws, the conversation was good and there were no Donald rants. Liz's younger brother, Peter, the priest was there, and he too was on his best behavior. He tends to have a lot of complaints about Our Holy Mother the Church, his employer, but he didn't voice them yesterday." So, we didn't have any lively discussions on politics or religion. How about you, Sandy?"

"I had a nice Sunday as well. My wife and I drove down to Hackett's Cove, where her parents still live, and took a picnic basket down by the little beach near their place. The water was still a bit chilly for swimming, but it was nice and warm for a picnic."

"And your leg, Sandy, all healed now?"

"Yep. Don't need that cane any more. It still pisses me off that they never caught that arsehole who shot me. Oh well, there's better things to think about than that. Water under the bridge".

"Good attitude."

"Grab yourself a coffee. I'll fill you in with the little information I have about the accident."

"I'm ready."

"A night watchman up at dockyard was found dead this morning. His name was Chesley Smith. They found him at the bottom of the hold on one the ships being repaired at the dry dock. A coal carrier called the *Port of Dover*. It looks like an accident, but the shipyard wants to make absolutely sure it was an accident. You know the routine, Harry. CYA."

"It's nice that some of these retired commissionaires get work in their retirement years, but a lot of them don't have the stamina or agility to do more than sit and watch out for trespassers. Did he have any family?"

"He was a retired commissionaire but enjoyed the occasional night watchman job. His wife died a few years back, and all his children seem to have ended up in Boston or around that area. I think one son ended up marrying a girl from St. John's and became a fisherman over there."

"All right, Sandy. Let me get sorted out here and I'll take one of the cruisers up to the North End. See what's what."

Two of the three patrol cars were sitting in the garage and Harry took one, filled it with gas from the station pump and headed down the hill to Barrington Street. As he drove north along Barrington Harry gazed at the long stretch of the harbour, up past the Acadia Sugar Refinery and the ferry terminal. A strong, salty breeze blew into the car from the open window. To Harry it smelled like exotic perfume.

He could see the Narrows and the bend in the harbour where the water skirted left past the coloured community of Africville before draining into Bedford Basin. Africville was snugly nestled into the Halifax side of the Basin shore, which gave it some protection from fierce harbour storms that made their way up through the Narrows.

Harry considered it probably one of the finest harbours in the world. He wasn't alone in his opinion. Deep, well protected from Atlantic storms, and crucial to the British war effort. And hopefully kept safe by the submarine nets stretching across the harbour entrance down by George's Island at the south end of Halifax.

It didn't take him more than twenty minutes to reach the dry dock. Harry was met there by a scarecrow of a man wearing a plaid shirt and dungarees. "Hello, Detective. My name's Ian, and I was instructed to bring you to the place where they found the night watchman."

"Very good, Ian. Lead on."

They proceeded down a short flight of wooden steps and had to weave their way through a maze of containers and stacks of lumber and other assorted containers of materials that were required for repairing sundry vessels.

"We don't get many outside visitors down here, and sometimes the dock gets overloaded with supplies."

"I can see that, Ian."

"Warren thought I should make sure you didn't get lost or step on any nails."

The gangplank was tilted at a 45-degree angle up to the main deck. Harry could see the edge of the main hold from the pier.

He quickly made his way up the gangplank and was greeted by Warren Smith.

"Good morning, Detective, and welcome aboard. My name's Warren Smith. I'm in charge of the Waterfront Security Commission." Smith was short, with shiny white hair combed straight back on his balding dome. His wire eyeglasses added to an official-looking demeanor. He impressed Harry with his impeccable grooming and starched white shirt, and especially his military posture. Harry guessed his age to be in his early sixties.

"Good morning, Warren. Call me Harry. It's a pleasure to meet you. Even if the circumstances are a little dreadful."

Warren's handshake was firm and dry. "Good morning, Harry."

"You remind me of my uncle," said Harry. "Were you also a military man?"

"In the navy all my life. Retired four years ago with the rank of Captain. Couldn't stand the idle life, so I bullied enough people for something to do and this is where I ended up. I'm here to help you in any way I can."

"I notice that the height of the lip around the hold isn't more than four feet. Isn't that a bit dangerous? I can see how someone could easily fall below. Especially an older person who was not familiar with the terrain."

"That's true, Harry. But that hold is usually covered with a lid. That's part of the reason this ship is in drydock. The ship's derrick needed to be repaired. But the hold lid was also damaged and needed to be replaced as well. That's why it was open yesterday."

"OK, Warren. show me where you found him."

"His name was Chesley Smith. No relation to me. From around Mahone Bay."

"Any family, Warren?"

"Not that we can determine. He had a room in the North End. The Maple Lodge. Pretty well kept to himself."

Warren led them to an outside flight of steps and down below water level to the hold. A heavy metal door gave them entrance to the empty hold.

"Watch your step, Harry. This is a coal carrier. What they call a collier. It was designed solely for carrying coal, and it's dirty down here. And coal dust can be slippery, especially when it's wet. As you can see there are still heaps of coal scattered around."

Harry took a careful look at the deck where the body lay covered with a tarp. He could see that the dust had been disturbed in this area. There were footprints all around and a small pool of dried blood. No one seemed to notice that some of the footprints veered off to the side and away from the body. There was no reason to poke around the scattered mounds of coal in the dark shadows. No reason at all to search for bombs.

Harry lifted the tarp and peered at the old man. *It looks like he died instantly, thank God*, Harry thought. The coroner who had examined him had determined that he had died of a broken neck sustained from the fall. "Poor fellow. What do you thing he was doing when he fell? Did he have to do rounds during the night?"

"No. All he had to do was to keep an eye on the gangplank and keep a lookout for anyone coming on board. There's nothing valuable on this kind of a boat, nothing to steal."

"What time did they find him, Warren?"

"It was around 6 AM. Two of the trimmers had arrived for duty. No holiday for them. The new lid has to be installed and the boat moved to the coal jetty. All this has to be done by tomorrow, because this boat is part of a convoy leaving here on Wednesday bound for England."

"They called the duty officer and he called the police. They had to rouse the on-duty coroner from his bed, and he eventually arrived to determine the cause of death. There was nothing they could do for the old fellow. As soon as you've had your look around, they will move the body to the morgue."

"I see a lot of footprints. Must've been a crowd down there?"

"The coroner had to go down below to examine the body so his footprints were there. But there were so many other footprints around the body that even if there was any suspicious evidence, we wouldn't have been able to find it."

"He sat up in the bridge, didn't he?"

"He did."

"It was probably comfortable up there. He wouldn't need to go outside unless something disturbed his attention. So, I guess therein lies the mystery. Why did he go outside?" It occurred to Harry, *Maybe he just went outside for a breath of fresh air? Maybe he had to go to the head? Or maybe he heard something?*

He followed Warren up the steep staircase to the bridge. Harry wondered what kind of a man would work on a coal carrier. He knew that trimmers had to work below decks during the loading and unloading operations. The load of coal had to be leveled before the boat was trimmed for sailing. *Was a trimmer the same kind of man who would work down in a mine, breathing coal dust?* Working on a grubby boat like this was not a sailor's dream job. Harry sighed. *Work is work, and everyone has bills to pay.*

There was a comfortable high-back stool in the bridge where the night watchman sat. It gave a good panoramic view over the prow and a lot of the port side dock area. There was also a chair at the rear of the bridge, but it didn't give the same view that the high-backed stool did. If the watchman sat there his view would be more limited.

It appeared that the night watchman was sitting on the stool when something caught his attention. He had poured himself a cup of tea and was halfway through his sandwich, which lay on a piece of waxed paper next to an apple. His jacket was still on the hook beside the cabin door.

"After those guys discovered the body, I locked up the bridge. No one has been in here since the old man. It's exactly how he left it."

"You did the right thing, Warren."

Harry and Warren climbed up the inner staircase to the top deck. They turned left along a short passage that ended at a five-foot railing just next to the pilot house door. Harry peered over the railing looking straight down a three-story drop to the bottom of the hold. The tarp-draped form lay directly below.

"It doesn't take much work to see that the old man fell from this point. The question is, why was he leaning over this railing?"

"I can't answer that, Harry. But I can tell you that the railing was designed the way it is to provide direct access from someone on this deck with someone directly below. The pilot house has a good panoramic view of the entire fore structure of the ship, but you can't communicate with someone directly below if you're inside the pilot house. It's a blind spot that you can't see from inside the pilot house. I guess he was leaning over too far and just lost his balance." *Or was pushed*, thought Harry.

To Harry's mind it seemed obvious that the old man was eating his late-night snack when something caught his attention. He might have heard something, or maybe he saw someone. But whatever it was, it interrupted his meal and he left his half-eaten sandwich to investigate. Next to a full mug of tea and a red McIntosh apple.

Harry tried to think like Sherlock Holmes, but determined as he was, he couldn't find any clues. All he had was the circumstantial evidence before him. And all he could do with that was apply a logical explanation that fit the situation. In spite of his nagging suspicions, he could not officially say a crime had been committed. The half-finished meal gnawed at Harry's mind, and he knew that it would stay there and fester until he came up with a logical explanation.

31

7 September 1916. Halifax.

IT WAS HOT. THE DAY AFTER THE CONVOY LEFT PORT, A tsunami of scalding western air descended on Halifax, which was as unusual as a polar bear sighting in Bedford Basin. If this had been Calgary, they would have called it a sirocco, a hot dry wind that comes in like a thief and leaves just as quickly. But this was the East Coast for goodness's sake, so what was that unwelcome hot air doing down here where it didn't belong? Haligonians were used to humid air, but this heat wave felt like someone had just opened the door to a blast furnace.

Harry had come into the station early. Might as well, after a sleepless night in the hot, humid air. He and Liz did have an overhead fan in their bedroom, but it was overtaxed and did nothing to alleviate their discomfort. By 5:00 AM Harry had had enough and drove to the station house, figuring he might as well do something useful rather than toss and turn in his uncomfortable bed any longer.

By 6:45 he was sitting at his desk, with his sleeves rolled up to the elbows and his tie at half-mast. He was eating a crispy McIntosh apple that had recently been harvested and he was reveling in the cool juiciness of it. A noisy old fan was aimed at his face, and all visible papers were either weighted down or stowed in drawers. He was ruminating on the meeting he and Sandy had a few weeks ago with the chief.

What suspicion, let alone evidence, was there, really, to spend much time looking for German agents in Halifax? But Harry had a naturally suspicious mind, and he enjoyed Mike's spy challenge by pretending he was solving a puzzle. All he needed were a few pieces of the puzzle and the possibility that the entire picture had an outline that he could fill in.

By the time Sandy arrived at 7:35 he had readjusted the fan so it faced away from the paperwork on his desk.

"Hey, old buddy, good morning to you. Grab yourself a cup of tea. Over in India where it is much hotter than here, and I mean all the time, they drink hot tea to cool off. They call it *chai*. And I guess it works."

"Good morning to you as well, Harry. It's not often I see you in here before me." Sandy also had his sleeves rolled up as high as he could get them.

"Couldn't sleep last night at all and finally decided to give Liz a break from all my tossing and turning and come in here where I wouldn't disturb anybody."

"Is that a fact?" said Sandy with a hint of suspicion in his voice. I thought you were just eager to solve Mike's challenge to find us some spies."

"Well, as a matter of fact, I've been thinking about that. I've read a few of those books about Sherlock Holmes. He was a very logical thinker. He examined his criminal investigations from every angle and was suspicious of anything that didn't make sense or didn't fit into the puzzle he was trying to solve. It's a good thing he didn't investigate the Bible, or he would have been burned at the stake by Our Holy Mother the Church."

Sandy shook his weary head. "There you go again, Harry. I sometimes think you'd be better off just admitting you're an agnostic, maybe even an atheist."

"Thought about that, Sandy. First of all, I wouldn't have a job. Or a wife. Or any friends in this city. Sometimes, though, I get carried away and can't help the occasional rant about the Church always telling us to accept the unknown as a mystery known only to God."

Harry turned the fan towards the middle of the room. He and Sandy sat at a large table over by an open window with a narrow view of the harbour. They could see the tail end of a fat tugboat hauling a small barge full of trimmed tree trunks. A puff of black-grey smoke floated straight up from the smoke stack without even a nudge from any sort of breeze.

"Where do we start, Harry?"

"I thought we should just write down any ideas, facts, beliefs and even rumours, even if they are outlandish. Even absurd. You've heard it said many times about crimes being solved and everyone saying, 'Who would have ever thought he did it? He was such a fine, outstanding person.'"

"Gotcha Harry. How about this? Six months ago, someone set fire to our House of Commons in Ottawa. It hasn't been proven, but there's a lot suspicion that it was the work of German saboteurs operating in Canada."

"Good start, Sandy. Good start. I like the way you think. I know very well that there are a lot of instances of sabotage south of the border, but I think we should limit our focus to Halifax and vicinity. It is our jurisdiction, and the only place where we can actually do anything." He was well aware of all the suspicious explosions aboard ships leaving New York and other eastern seaboard destinations bound for England and France. That might be a consideration for Halifax, although the convoys leaving here were a drop in the bucket compared to the United States.

"What I am thinking, Sandy, is that we should start by seeing if there are any instances of sabotage against ships leaving on convoys from Halifax. I'm wondering about that ship that left in the last convoy and blew up at sea a few days later."

"It was called the S.S. *William Severance*, Harry. There was a military investigation, but I don't think anything came of it. Nothing I'm aware of, in any case."

"Well, I think we should look into it a little further. We don't have any facilities like Black Tom to worry about, so we don't need to waste our time looking in that direction. And the fire in Ottawa—I don't think there is much to think about there unless a suspect turns up who has a connection to someone in Halifax.

"Speaking of Halifax, I have a guy I know who keeps a lookout for German spies. He's not much of an investigator, but he does haunt places where furtive people hang out. If there are any enemy agents skulking about, Packy would be the most likely person I know to encounter someone acting suspicious. Maybe I should pay more attention to what he tells me. Even nudge him a bit."

"Not really much to start an investigation with, is it Harry?"

"Nope. But as Confucius says, 'A journey of a thousand miles starts with a single step.' Let's begin with the S.S. *William Severance*. Oh! And add that collier to that list. There's something that bothers me about that night watchman falling to his death."

32

9 Sept 1916. North Atlantic.

THE CONVOY HAD LEFT HALIFAX THREE DAYS AGO, ON Wednesday, and had made excellent progress enjoying good weather and calm seas, with four British cruisers escorting the fleet. There were eighteen ships altogether. The cruisers darted about like a pack of shepherd dogs minding their flock of sheep, always on the lookout for wolves.

It was just past 7 AM. The kitchen staff were in the middle of cleaning up after breakfast. Then, a whine and a crack, and a great explosion roared. A rupture on the port rivet seam, water gushing through the rift. Then another blast, this time on the starboard hull. Another rupture.

Sirens and screams. Nobody injured, but lots of smoke as the coal started to bake. The list to starboard took control and got more pronounced as the minutes sped by.

Faint shouts of "Abandon ship!" These were more like gasps of alarm, as there was no command to abandon ship. That order had not yet been issued. Flames began to rage below deck as the list to starboard became more inclined. The danger zone had not been reached yet, at least not in the captain's mind.

The seas were heaving, but they were gentle swells and not crashing waves. More like an enormous beating heart. One cruiser had left to help the stricken ship and a nearby freighter was closing in to help.

No one was in the water. The *Port of Dover* had launched two lifeboats and the nearby freighter, *Francine*, had done the same. Under the very tight gaze of the captain, crewmen started climbing into the nearest lifeboat. More than half of the twelve-man crew were aboard the first lifeboat when there was a sudden lurch. The prow of the *Port of Dover* crashed violently down to port, and the wash tore the second lifeboat from its mooring.

The lifeboat from the *Francine* had just reached the first lifeboat. The remaining crew members managed to reach this second lifeboat without any serious injury. The captain, as was his duty, was the last person to step off the shivering gangplank.

They had almost reached the *Francine* when the *Port of Dover* slipped beneath the waves. There was no big explosion, no dramatic upending like drawings depicting the sinking of the *Titanic* four years ago. She just rolled a bit and disappeared on her maiden voyage down to Davy Jones' locker.

33

21 Nov 1917. New York.

"IT BEGINS, AIMÉ." ALPHONSE NEEDED TO ACKNOWLEDGE
the moment. At precisely 8 AM on Wednesday morning, eight
trucks loaded with TNT and guncotton arrived with an escort of
five police cars with flashing lights. They pulled up to the loading
area in front of the dirty grey *Mont Blanc*, sporting its war colour.

From one of the police cars emerged a small, sweaty man with
a red face and a shiny bald head. Greasy long strands of dark hair
coiled around his ears. Edward Flower was the assistant maritime
inspector in the French government's office and its local agent. He
approached the gangplank with trepidation. He was not looking
forward to meeting Aimé Le Médec.

"Welcome aboard, Mr. Flower," Jean greeted him in perfect
English. "Captain Le Médec awaits you in the wheelhouse."

Flower was a little startled when he shook hands with the captain. He was expecting a taller person than this diminutive man
who stood in front of him with such a serious expression. But
Le Médec did indeed have the look of authority that would be
needed to command this ship.

"I, too, welcome you aboard. We have a total crew of thirty-
nine souls on this ship, and we are all wondering why the *Mont
Blanc* was chosen for this duty when our sister ships, the *Antilles*
and the *Abd el-Kader* are both faster ships and better maintained."

Flower replied, but his heart wasn't in it. He knew how many times guilty people relied on the old excuse, *I was just following orders.*

"If it's any consolation, Captain Le Médec, it was not my decision. The decision was made by my boss who represents the French government in the United States. It's my duty to carry out these orders. To quote the great English poet, Lord Tennyson, *Ours not to reason why; ours but to do or die.* I believe, as you do, that our duty is to follow orders."

"And yet, Mr. Flower, you concealed from us the fact that we would be carrying ammunition. You knew before we even set sail from France what our cargo was to be. Do you not think that we should have been consulted beforehand, considering that our cargo would consist entirely of explosives?"

"Would it have made any difference, Captain? The needs of the French army are dire. They need as many supplies as we can provide. Did you know that for months now, I've dispatched as many as four merchant ships a week back to Bordeaux, all of them laden with American manufactured ammunition? Even that is not enough. Ordinarily the *Mont Blanc* would never have been called upon to carry such a volatile load. But we're short of ships, so we have no choice but to use what we can get our hands on."

Flower's explanation did little to alleviate Le Médec's growing unease. "I've never transported explosives before, Mr. Flower. It's not just the German U-boats that pose a deadly danger to us. We could run into extremely dangerous weather, or we might simply nudge a pier too hard and set off an explosion. I pray to God we will arrive safely in Bordeaux, but I've a very bad feeling about this voyage." If only he knew how fateful his premonitions would turn out.

34

11 September 1916. Halifax.

HARRY ARRIVED AT THE STATION JUST AFTER EIGHT, which was a little later than usual. His oyster eyes told the story. He had greeted the day with a bit of a headache, probably caused by downing too much of that red wine at last night's festivities. And he really hadn't needed those two brandies to finish the evening.

Sunday had been one of the summer's best weather days by far. A welcome guest too great to say no to, especially after the stifling heat wave. Liz was up at the crack of dawn, and by nine o'clock she had packed a picnic fit for a king. Leftover chicken breasts and egg sandwiches, their daughter Milly's favourite. A crusty loaf from Ben's Bakery, ham slices and a simple salad of lettuce, cucumber, tomatoes and French dressing. A few bottles of lemonade, and hidden at the bottom of the hamper four bottles of Oland's finest for Harry and Larry.

Larry was Harry's oldest friend since grade three, and they were going to meet Larry and his wife Agnes at Hubbard's beach around 11:30 for a swim and a picnic. Larry's son Andy was a year older than Milly, so the two would have each other for company. They had taken in the ten o'clock mass at St. Thomas' and were well on their way towards Hubbard's by 10:45, taking the treacherous St. Margaret's Bay Road with all its twists and hairpin curves.

The weather had been spectacular, the water temperature

perfect, and the picnic a huge success. Agnes had celebrated her 35th birthday on Friday. The birthday weekend didn't end until Sunday evening, when Larry and Agnes were invited back to Harry's to finish off the day with a birthday cake and ice cream. And a bottle of champagne, and a few too many chasers afterward. Agnes, their guest of honour, had not been drinking much, so she drove the family car home.

"You look like shit!" Sandy gave him a little pat on the shoulder. "When my father, God bless him, woke up like that, he always had two raw eggs in a glass with a shot of Worchester sauce. Said it did wonders for a hangover."

"Ugh."

"I haven't got any eggs here at the station, Harry, but I do have a big pot of steaming tea."

The station house was on the north side of Citadel Hill, and they could see a long stretch of the harbour looking across to Dartmouth. A lone schooner under sail was heading outbound toward the Atlantic under swirls of dark grey morning fog.

The main floor had a corridor off to the left where the chief's office was located behind an opaque glass window. Harry and Sandy shared a raised floor three feet above the front counter, where the duty sergeant was filling out paperwork. A low railing kept them safe from falling.

"Have you seen this morning's *Chronicle Herald*, Sandy? There's a report of another ship exploding at sea for no reason. They didn't say much in the paper."

"Way ahead of you Harry. We had a call from Warren Smith from Waterfront Security."

"That's the chap that showed me around the boat on Monday. Where the night watchman fell into the hold. It's officially an accident, but I have my doubts. What did he want?"

"Said that the boat that sank in the convoy was the *Port of Dover*."

"Jesus, Mary and Joseph. Can't be a coincidence, can it? I'll give him a call, no point in going up there on such a lousy day." Coincidence my foot. Only the friggin' Catholic Church says God works in mysterious ways. And this didn't happen by the hand of God."

"You're right, Harry. The S.S. *William Severance* last month and now the *Port of Dover*. Two ships that left Halifax and exploded a few days later. Do you think there could be a connection"?

"Mike is always sayin' that the devil is in the details. You know what that phrase means, don't you Sandy?"

"Sort of. Enlighten me."

Harry stood up and stretched his arms high above his head. "It's an old saying, Sandy. Paying attention to small things has big rewards."

Sandy slapped the table. "Excellent! Let's make a list of all the facts we know for certain. If we have enough pieces that fit together, we just might be able to complete a jigsaw."

"No question, Sandy. We will make that list without any pre-judgements, but we still need to follow our suspicions and heed our gut feelings."

"I'm on board. How about this? One list of facts. Provable facts. And a second list of things and persons of interest. Coincidences."

"I'm feeling better already, Sandy."

35

15 Sept 1916. New York.

BEN HAD ARRIVED BY TRAIN THE NIGHT BEFORE, AND now found himself in a sleezy hotel in lower Brooklyn. He was cautious about staying too near the German community. Things had heated up after the Black Tom explosion in July.

While the United States did not have a unified federal agency to investigate crimes of national importance like Black Tom, they did have several investigative agencies at the state and local level, which did their best to unravel the details of the explosion. Their separate investigations suffered in areas where a unified effort would have succeeded, such as the sharing of information. All to the advantage of the saboteurs.

One such investigation was headed by New York City Police Department inspector Thomas J. Tunney. Tunney was an Irish-American veteran of the NYPD who had a deep knowledge of bombs from his time tracking anarchist groups around the turn of the century. In 1916 he was head of the NYPD bomb squad, which by then had turned its focus on foreign agents.

In the aftermath of Black Tom, he formed a task force to investigate allegations of a German spy ring being run out of New York. His Irish ancestry helped him stay closely connected with the Irish community, giving him the opportunity to build a network of informants who often provided information, if not rumours, of sabotage activities. He had an idea of who might be behind the brazen sabotage of Black Tom.

Ben was meeting with Paul Koeing in a dingy bar on the outskirts of the Bowery. Koeing had insisted on this bar because it was out of the way and had little traffic this late on Friday evening. He was dressed in his customary attire of a long black raincoat and black fedora.

Koeing had just finished his third cigarette, smoked down to the quick as evidenced by his nicotine-stained fingers. He gulped down the dregs of his dark ale and ordered two more.

"One for my friend here and another for me."

"Thanks, Paul. It's good to see you again," Ben said with a wry smile as they shook hands.

"It's not the grandest spot for a get together, but the beer's not bad. As I alluded to you on the telephone, I am being watched by secret servicemen, so it's not good for your well-being to be seen in my company." He said this with some flippancy, but there were dark undertones that couldn't conceal a lurking dread.

Ben huddled close to Paul and whispered, "I heard that von Rintelen went back to Germany. Was he also being watched?"

Paul crouched closer as his eyes searched for suspicious persons. "People in power back in Germany were not happy with his performance here in New York. They knew the authorities here had suspicions of his involvement with Black Tom. He was being carefully observed. I am not sure if he was ordered back to Germany, but he left here by boat in early August bound for England."

"So, Paul, he is safe back in Germany?"

"I wish that was so, but I've heard, unofficially, that he has been arrested in Southampton and is now locked up in a British prison."

"What about Scheele? Is he still in business?"

"Ben, that's the other thing. He was indicted for making

bombs, and he fled to Cuba. More repercussions from the Black Tom explosion. They somehow connected him to that event."

Ben expressed regrets about these developments, but he was more concerned about the support he was likely to receive for his ongoing efforts in Halifax. "Tell me Paul," he said leaning forward, "what's happened to the manufacture of our product?"

"We have quite a supply. Well hidden, as you would expect. But no new production is in the works, and won't be for a while. Do you still have stock?"

"We've enough for three or four targets, but if we could get another shipment, that would carry us through until next summer."

"Listen Ben, things are a little tense here in New York. The authorities are aware of my association with von Rintelen and I'm sure they suspect me of having some contact with Scheele. They don't have enough to tie me to anything yet but if they keep digging, I'm sure they will find something."

"Are you in any danger, Paul?"

"No. Not right now. But I have to be careful. I could probably get you a box of cigars, but it might take a couple of months. Our activities have been cut back as more and more scrutiny is being applied to stevedores. Random searches of men loading convoy-bound ships, that sort of thing."

"We're seeing that in Halifax as well. Not as much as here, but the dockyard authorities seem to have a more watchful eye than they used to. And I've learned that the Halifax Police have started a low-level investigation to ascertain if there is any substance to rumours of German agents being active in Halifax. It's only two cops doing the research and they have no evidence at all. Only suspicions."

"All I can say, Ben, is be careful. It's not going to be easy for you and I to maintain contact for the time being. I'll get you another shipment whenever I can, but we will just have to wait and see what happens in the coming months."

"Anything will help."

"One other thing, Ben, I have a loyal contact who works as a clerk at the National City Bank of New York. His responsibilities make him privy to the cargos and destinations of ships bound for Europe. To help the Allied cause. That is very useful for our operations here in New York and New Jersey."

"Well, that's great for you, Paul, but what good's that information for me in Canada?"

"I was just getting to that, Ben." Koeing lit yet another cigarette, took a big gulp of beer, and looked Ben straight in the eye. "Sometimes he comes across a ship that's taking on cargo in New York and sailing to Halifax to join a convoy heading to Europe."

"So? What's our involvement in Halifax?"

Koeing leaned in so close to Ben they could be mistaken for lovers. Ben could almost taste his beery breath. Koeing whispered, "There's a ship arriving from Portsmouth on the 25th of September. She's taking on a load of ammunition in New York and is booked to join a convoy leaving Halifax on the 4th of October. That ship is called HMS *Justica*. Security is so tight we won't have any chance of planting any charges here in New York."

"I can assure you, Paul, with the heightened security we have in Halifax, we're not going to able to do anything you won't be able to do in New York. And if her cargo has already been loaded in New York, we wouldn't have any reason to even approach this ship. She would be anchored in Bedford Basin, and that puts her out of reach."

Koeing smiled. "I've got a secret for you, Ben. Hardly anyone knows this, but this ship will be loading a couple of crates of highly explosive TNT while it is in Halifax. It's a secret consignment being supplied by the Canadian authorities. As you know, Canada is at war with Germany. It is not a neutral country like the U.S. So, this shipment cannot be exposed as being supplied by Canada. It all has to do with maintaining the neutrality of the convoy. That's why all the secrecy."

"That's great news, Paul. Tell me what I need to know."

36

18 Sept 1916. Halifax.

"IT'S ALWAYS NICE TO HAVE A BEER WITH YOU, HARRY."

Harry had left the office around 3:30 on this slow Monday afternoon. Not his normal leaving time, but his 'undercover source,' Packy, said he might have some gossip for him. They were sitting at a table by the window in the Pig. The big window was glazed over but was letting in a lot of diffused, weary light from the late afternoon sun. It gave the room a tired feel.

"My pleasure, Packy."

"You going to join me, or would the missus frown on you coming home with beer on your breath?"

"I think I just might have a pint. My wife is not the kind of a person who frowns on such trivial things as coming home from the pub with beer on my breath. It is a rare event, in any case. Liz and I have been known to have a cocktail before supper."

Billy, the bartender, brought them two pints of Oland's. He nodded at Harry. "A little early for you, Harry?"

"It's a business meeting, Billy. Packy and I have business to discuss."

"Well, it's still early, so you have the place all to yourselves. I will leave you in peace."

"What have you got, Packy? Somebody else talking about blowing up the submarine net?"

"You may laugh, my friend. I've heard what I've heard. You do remember, though, that I mentioned that short guy with the red hair? He was with the military chap. And if they weren't talking about submarine nets, they were talking about something suspicious."

"I remember what you said."

"Well, guess what Harry? I saw him the other night. His bright red curly hair and big shiny forehead are a dead giveaway. And maybe I could add his surly face, as well."

"Where, Packy? Where'd you see him? In the Pig again?"

"Nope. It was in Harriet's." Everyone knew Harriet's brothel was a den of loose conversation and was frequented by every sailor visiting the port of Halifax. Not to mention a lot of other unsavory characters in the port city.

"Ah! Harriet's."

"You know I have a girlfriend who lives there. Rita. We're pals. Sometimes I crash there. Mostly I live with my old Mom, but sometimes I have a wee bit too much to drink and I know I need to spare the old lady my inebriated presence."

"You've a heart of gold, Packy. This information you have. Anything to do with Rita?"

"As a matter of fact, it does." Harry takes a long swig of his pint and drags his cuff across his whiskered face. "There was a rowdy customer in Harriet's the night I slept over. Not Rita's customer, but he made so much commotion everyone in the house was quite aware of his presence."

A few months ago, Danny was booked to see Rita but got arrested before he could make it to the brothel.

"Elly. He was with Elly. As you know, there's a back room where customers can wait, and sometimes you can get a drink there. And sometimes there's other patrons waiting as well."

"That a fact, Packy? I'm not supposed to know that. Not in my official capacity."

"Yeah, I know that. But life here in Halifax consists of laws that are enforced and laws that exist but are not acknowledged."

"Or exist and are acknowledged with a nod and a wink," said Harry, as he took a big swig of his Oland's.

"This chap obviously had too much to drink, Harry. Elly and him were having a wee tipple before the main event, as it were. There were two other patrons there as well. Couple of merchant marines. Americans, they were. Discussing the war and America's neutrality. Wondering when the U.S. was ever going to declare war with Germany."

"Lots of people having that conversation, Packy. Me included."

"Yeah. But our friend gets all snarly and pipes up that that Americans are supplying war materials to Britain so they are in cahoots with the British. Therefore, they're already on the side of England and against Germany." Packy paused long enough to take a huge swallow.

He continued," It turns out that our friend has an Irish background, and as you know there's a lot of hatred in Ireland for the British. It's no secret who they would like to see win this war. I learned later that our friend's name was Danny Sullivan. He starts calling the two merchant marines arseholes. Then they get into it. There's a sense that Danny Sullivan is the instigator of the ruckus, so Mick, the bouncer, tosses him out. Fortunately, he doesn't come back."

"All right, Packy. I understand. First you thought you heard this guy, Danny Sullivan, talking about blowing up submarine nets. That made him a suspicious person in your eyes. Now you hear news about him from a second-hand conversation. Maybe even from a third-hand conversation if you heard it from Rita, who heard it from Elly."

"So?"

"I grant you that Danny Sullivan seems to support Germany in this conflict. And I appreciate your reporting to me, Packy. I really do. But what we have is only circumstantial evidence. Our suspicions might grow stronger, but without evidence we've nothing to act on. Don't get me wrong. I want to hear about any other suspicious behaviours you might come across. Gossip and rumours can often serve as good foundation to bolster a bona fide case when facts and evidence are discovered."

"OK, Gov. I get it. One more for the road?"

"I'll get you another pint, but I gotta run. Take care. And thanks for your information. We'll be in touch."

37

30 September 1916. Halifax.

IT WAS EARLY AFTERNOON ON THE LAST DAY OF September. The bright sunlight was welcome, but the strong harbour wind blowing up the face of Citadel Hill had a sharp bite to it. Tucked into the lee of a natural berm below the old fort, Ben and Danny looked down the grassy slope towards the whitecaps crowning the water rushing into Halifax harbour.

They had a panoramic view of Halifax and the whole length of the harbour, way past the sandbar that was McNab's Island. All the way out to Chebucto Head and the Atlantic. They were watching the HMS *Justica* make its way up past George's Island, on its way past the dockyards to the Narrows, where the elbow of the harbour curved left and emptied into Bedford Basin.

Ben was closely observing the ship's progress with a pair of binoculars. He could clearly see that the HMS *Justica* had a two-story bridge set in the exact middle of this 32,234 ton ship. A row of eight windows stretched from one curved side, across the front to the other curved side. There were three crane arms over the fore hold and another three crane arms over the aft hold.

The HMS *Justica* had already been boarded by the harbour authorities and had passed their inspection. The harbour pilot was now in charge, and he was guiding the ship along the Dartmouth shoreline at the maximum harbour speed limit of four miles an hour. If Ben had any doubt about the cargo, he was reassured by the red flag flying from the masthead. A red flag signalled to all traffic in the harbour that this ship was carrying explosives. A mandatory warning to stay clear. The submarine nets would be closing in the next two hours. If the ship had arrived later than four o'clock, it would have been denied entry to the harbour and forced to weigh anchor by George's Island.

"Are you prepared for tomorrow night, Danny?"

"I'm ready for Freddy, as my old man used to say," a hint of amusement in his voice. He couldn't help himself. It was his nature. *No frigging way he was going to be as serious as Ben seemed to be all the time. That guy could've been a priest. Imagine getting a penance from him in the confessional.*

"Let's get serious, Danny. I want you to pay close attention to what we are going to do here. Do not fuck with me, you understand?" Ben was a no-nonsense kind of man. Tall and angular and not an ounce of fat. Someone who would do his job and by God, he expected you do to your job as well. A smile did not easily stick to his face.

"Fine. You're the boss. Just tell me what to do."

"This ship, the *Justica*, is leaving here Wednesday joining a convey heading over to England. The ship was loaded with ammunition in New York before arriving in Halifax. That's why it's flying that red flag. Not many people know this, but it'll leave its mooring in the Basin early Monday morning and dock at Pier 15. There it will load two pallets of highly volatile TNT. It's a special consignment arranged by the Canadian government. That's why it wasn't loaded in New York. There's no room in either hold, so these pallets will be lashed to rigging near the ship's prow."

"Isn't that dangerous loading them topside?" Danny ventured his concern.

"The TNT is wrapped in thick rubber and encased in heavy duty canvas to keep it dry, even in heavy seas. Each bundle is protected by a wooden crate to protect it and keep it from bumping around. The only real danger of an explosion would be from a fire.

I've managed to include you in the work crew that will load these pallets sometime on Monday. After the loading is complete, the ship will return to its anchor in the Basin in preparation for the convoy's departure on Wednesday. There will tighter than normal security during the loading at Pier 15. All because of all those bombs being planted on ships leaving American ports."

Danny hacked a smoker's cough and spit as he lighted another cigarette. "Damn fags" he muttered under his breath.

"The crew of the *Justica* will operate the cranes, but we will be required to guide the cargo onto the ship. Our job is to secure it tightly into place. Which will require some carpentry work from our crew. We'll have to build the braces that hold the pallets tightly against the ship rails and make sure the canvas tarps are secured against raging seas.

"We will be closely watched by an inspector from the admiralty on Monday, so we won't be able to plant anything on that ship. And that's where you and I come in." Ben spoke in a low voice even though there was no one in sight. You and I are going to have to get into the storage shed sometime Sunday night and do our duty for the Kaiser. Danny, just don't let me down."

*   *   *

"Come on Packy, let's walk over to the Public Gardens. I've seen enough of this old fort. It'll do us a world of good to get a bit of exercise. Then we can have a drink over at the Nellie without feeling too guilty about it." Rita and Packy had taken a taxi to the fort on top of Citadel Hill. The star-shaped fort had been built by the British in the 19th century to serve as a command post for harbour defence works. It also served as a garrison for British soldiers stationed in this lonely outpost. Now it was more of a tourist attraction.

"Speak for yourself, Rita. I would never feel guilty about having a drink at the Lord Nelson Hotel." Packy was not an old man, but he had all the characteristics of one. He shuffled more than he walked. And his head always seemed to be bent forward, as if he was a hunchback. And he always seemed to need a shave. But his eyes glistened with the mischievousness of a younger man.

They left the eastern entrance and headed clockwise on the gravel road that sloped downward toward the gardens. It was Rita's idea that they should *do something* on such a beautiful day and not hang around and *do nothing* like they did so many times in their lives.

As they walked on the gravel path around the bend of the hill they had a magnificent view of the south end of the city, all the way to Point Pleasant Park and out to the Atlantic Ocean. "Hold on a minute," Packy suddenly whispered to Rita. "See those two men below us? That guy with the red hair. I recognize him. Don't make any noise. I don't want him to see us."

"Does he know you, Packy?"

"I don't think so, but I don't want him to see me in any case." At that moment the taller of the two men turned slightly toward the redhead, and Packy could see he was peering through a set of binoculars. He seemed to be focused on a freighter heading past George's Island.

"I recognize those two, Rita. I've seen them together before down at the Pig's Revenge. That shorter guy with the curly red hair—I would recognize him anywhere. And the taller one, he looks like a military guy to me. Let's get out of their sight." Packy had a momentary inclination to tell Harry about this sighting but decided he wouldn't bother Harry until he had more substantial facts. Evidence, Harry had said.

38

1 October 1916. Halifax.

PIER 15 WAS A SMALL AND HARDLY USED LOADING DOCK located near the bottom of Duffis Street, not far from the ferry terminal. The area around the dock was littered with broken dock equipment that somebody would mend someday, whenever that time arrived. There was a solid corrugated shed that was used mostly for long term storage and even then, the items stored there consisted of old wooden pallets, ropes and rusty pipes. It wasn't a place that was deemed a high security risk. The strategic thinking was that this out-of-the-way shack would not attract any attention, especially to a saboteur looking for a ready target.

Because of that factor, the powers in charge deemed it the ideal place to stash the eight pallets of high explosives for just a few days. There were no lifting cranes on the dock, but that would not be a problem because the HMS *Justica* had six cranes of its own. The pallets would be loaded onto the *Justica* on Monday afternoon, before she made her way back to her anchorage in the Basin in preparation for the convoy leaving early on Wednesday.

Ben and Danny had arrived at the site just before midnight to scout out the terrain. They watched the night watchman do two rounds, passing the shed twice. It was close to 2 AM when they finally made their way along the unused railway spur that no longer serviced this dock. It was overgrown with weeds, and unlit.

It didn't take much effort to climb over the mostly broken fence that snaked around the back of the storage shed.

There was a half moon that night, but scudding clouds allowed scant illumination.

"Be careful," Ben said, "there are a lot of dry branches and old wood that will signal our presence if you step on a piece." Ben felt good about this operation. He knew the only way they were going to plant their six pipe bombs on the HMS *Justica* was to get them hidden inside the crates. They would never be able plant the bombs on the ship otherwise. Sometimes luck is as good as the best laid plans. Ben was a firm believer in luck. You couldn't count on it, but you sure as hell should welcome it if it came your way. Good old Lady Luck.

Danny carried a small tote bag with their tools and the primed bombs. Each bomb was about six inches tall and as thick around as a cigar. They had been primed to explode in sixty hours. Their arsenal also included strong tape, pliers, a small saw, a hammer and a bolt cutter. And a used lock identical to the one securing the side door to the shed.

They made their way carefully around to the water side of the shed. The door to the shed was shaded from a nearby dock light by an upended section of old dock that had been braced against an empty coal storage bin.

Danny whispered, "Are we OK Ben? I've been looking out for that night watchman, but I haven't seen anything." He felt a bit nervous exposed here on the open dock. "What if someone sees us?"

"Just fucking listen, Danny. I told you before that the night watchman doesn't walk past this spot more than once every two hours. I'm sure he doesn't give this place more than a glance as long as he sees that the door is closed." Danny secretly wondered what the watchman would do if he noticed the lock was missing. "Your night vision has kicked in, so we don't need a flashlight. Stop worrying."

Ben creeped along the side of the shed and reached the door. He used the bolt cutter on the lock and opened the door, which only complained with a faint creak. He signaled Danny to join him inside the shed. Before he pulled the door shut behind them, he managed to fit the broken lock into the clasp holding the lock in such a way that from a distance the lock looked to be nicely in place. It would not hold up to close scrutiny, but Ben was confident the watchman would not bother much with an inspection. *It'll be his last inspection if he does*, thought Ben.

The eight skids of explosives, in two rows, faced the overhead door. Each skid had two wooden crates, one on top of the other, secured with a metal band front to back. The slats of each crate were spaced far enough apart that the canvas covering was visible. The sides of the two crates were their objective tonight.

"Let's try those two crates on the front pallet. There's enough light to see by, and I can use this flashlight sparingly if I need to. See if you can pry out the nails enough so we can get a grip on them. We need to pry off the bottom slat without breaking it. Nice and slow, Danny, easy does it. We have lots of time. Try not to scratch the wood. We don't want anyone inspecting these crates too closely."

Ben went over to the small window to keep a lookout for the watchman. This window was their source of light. Danny started with the first slat and managed to pry up four of the six nails holding the slat in place. Two on each end of the slat and two in the middle. He had some difficulty with the nails on the left side, mainly because they were in a dark corner.

"Ben, I need some light here—I can't see what I'm doing."

Ben took a last good look around the pier and went over to Danny's side. "I'll hold this light for you. It's intentionally weak but it'll do." Danny had no problem with the first nail, but the other one was a bit bent, and he started getting a bit frustrated. Ben turned out the light. "Take five, Danny."

Ben went back to the window. "Quiet, Danny. I hear something. Don't move."

He could see the night watchman in the distance. He appeared to be heading for the shed. *Be careful, old man, I'd hate to be feeding you to the fishes tonight.* The watchman reached the other side of the empty coal bin. He stopped and fiddled with his zipper. Taking a piss. He farted and finished his call to nature and continued along his route. Ben sighed. *Luck is on my side tonight, but I guess she was also on your side, old man. You came close to dying, my friend.*

Ben shone the light again for Danny, and this time he managed to remove the last stubborn nail. He removed the slat, which was about ten inches wide. He taped the first bomb to the left of center and the other bomb to the right of center. He was very careful to replace the slat back in place and align the nail holes exactly. There was enough slack in the canvas surrounding the explosives for the pipe bombs to snuggle, and when the nails were hammered back in place there was no evidence the crate had been tampered with.

Danny managed the same operation on the lower crate in less time than he did on the first. They had been in the shed for just over half an hour.

"Good work, Danny. You did an excellent job. Time to go." It had been thirty minutes since the watchman passed by. "I don't think he will be back for at least another half hour, but let's keep it as quiet as we can."

They left the shed and closed the door without any noise. Ben replaced the lock he destroyed with the spare he brought with him. *There will be some confusion in the morning when they try to open this lock and discover that their keys don't fit. But I'm sure they will figure out something*, thought Ben.

39

26 Nov 1917. New York.

"GOOD LORD, JEAN, THEY ARE PUTTING US IN UNBEARABLE danger," Aimé raged at his First Officer. They were standing on the fantail of the *Mont Blanc* as it jutted out over the rudder and the cold water below. "The risk of explosion is outrageous. Do you not agree with me, Jean?" he fumed, as his white knuckles tried to strangle the railing.

"Yes, Captain, I agree. If it wasn't war time and if France's needs weren't so dire, I would protest to the highest authorities. My only consolation is that if it was not for this war, this cargo would never have been authorized. Patriotism overrides our fear, as it must." Jean's gaze faltered as he looked away from Aimé. He had voiced a scripted response, but his words betrayed an inner feeling of dread.

Since the previous Wednesday the entire below-deck cargo space of the *Mont Blanc* had been filled to the brim with guncotton, picric acid and TNT. When the carpenters had finished lining every metal space below deck with lumber, they built specially constructed wooden magazines with no iron features to separate each type of explosive. Even the bars closing the holds had been covered with tarred cloth. The holds themselves had then been hermetically sealed to close off access altogether.

"Ah, yes. Patriotism. The reason we fight. On our side. And on the other side. And God, Jean. Don't forget He fights on the other side as well." Aimé took a deep breath and let go of the railing. "Forgive me, my friend. My pent-up feelings and frustrations sometimes get the better of me."

Back home in France Aimé was always very relaxed with his family and friends. They knew him as a man with an inquisitive mind and strong determination. His house was decorated with souvenirs from exotic ports of call—native masks, spears and baubles. At sea he was more reserved and aloof, and insisted on doing things 'by the book.'

The personnel file his employer kept on him described him as an active and conscientious officer. Yet, it was also said of him by people who he sailed with that he was a moody but likable man. A competent rather than a brilliant sailor. He was a captain under whose command sailors felt confident in serving.

"Aimé, you only express what the whole crew feels. Altogether we are forty souls on a suicide mission. Do you think there are any among us any who hasn't thought of a loved one back home in France? Anyone that doesn't fear that they might never see that person again? A wife. A child. A parent. A friend. We are all in this together, and I know you are going to do your best to get us home. I'm sure you have noticed how cautious those stevedores were, wearing linen clothes over their boots to avoid sparks when they walked on the metal decks. I'll bet they feel relieved they are not part of this crew."

"You're right, Jean. We're all in this together. I still can't help feeling that we are being used. Between you and me, I don't trust that Edward Flowers. Apparently, it was his idea to telegraph the office in France and advise them there that the weight limit of cargo on the *Mont Blanc* had not been exceeded, and that there was room on the outside decks for more cargo. As a consequence, the stevedores will start loading barrels of benzol on our main deck beginning this afternoon. As soon as all the holds below have been completely sealed, I want you to be in charge to make sure everything is stowed safely in place. Can you see to this, Jean?"

"Yes, Captain. Let's just get on with it, shall we?"

40

2 October 1916. Halifax.

EARLY ON MONDAY MORNING BEN AND DANNY JOINED two other stevedores on the loading dock. They would form the four-man crew that would load the pallets onto the deck of the HMS *Justica* and secure them in place for the Atlantic crossing the next morning.

Three other men faced them. One was the crew foreman, Bernie Frost, a crusty old sod if ever there was one. Frost was a big bruiser of a guy who acted like he had a low tolerance for things going wrong. He was accompanied by a military officer and a civilian gentleman.

Frost addressed the crew. "Good morning, men. This is Sergeant Preston and this is Mr. Barr. Sergeant Preston represents the military's interests. Mr. Barr is the Halifax agent for this here ship. He is going to inspect your work here today and report back to the ship's owners when everything is safely secured for your voyage on Wednesday."

Ben approached Frost and said in a threatening voice, "Good day, Mr. Frost. I'm wondering when we will be getting started. I don't see any ship in sight."

"We were expecting the ship to be here by now, but there were some unforeseen problems. She won't be weighing anchor until noon or so. I expect her to be docked here around one or one thirty. In the meantime, you and your crew can start lugging those crates over here. We'll load them when the ship is docked. And don't worry, you will be paid for all your time."

"Danny, you and the boys can wheel that dolly over to the shed. I'll go over to the office and get the key to the side door," Ben said in all sincerity.

"Never mind," said Frost in his gruff voice. "I have the keys. Let's go." He went over to the shed but couldn't open the lock. "What the hell? Goddam keys don't fit. Neither one." He kept fiddling with the keys, as if he could force them to work. "These were the only keys in the drawer, so they have to be the right ones."

He heard a little snicker and snarled, "Fuck off. Go get me a crow bar, you barmy bastard."

Ray, one of the stocky crew, brought him a large crowbar. Bernie used it to snap off the useless lock, which he then tossed into the empty coal bin.

They opened the big overhead door and found the four-wheeled dolly nosed inside. The crates were fairly heavy, and it took all four of the strong-backed men to load each one onto the dolly. The dolly could not hold more than two crates at a time. Even if it could, it would be too heavy to pull across the dirt surface on its iron wheels. Four trips would be required.

It took the crew almost an hour and a half to get the eight crates to the waterside, but it was just as well, because the HMS *Justica* was just arriving at the dock when they had finished.

Once the ship was berthed the loading began. Each crate had two thick rope handles, which the ship's overhead cranes hooked onto and lowered onto the deck of the ship. Space had been made for four crates on either side of the forward deck, since there was no room in the hold.

Ben and Danny made their way up the gangplank to guide the crates into place. The other two stevedores stayed on the dock to make sure the crates were properly attached to the ship's crane.

One of the ship's crewmen greeted the two stevedores and showed them where and how the crates were to be placed. "Those crates are a bit bigger than we were expecting, but we'll fit them OK. We've got chains and lots of wood to secure them safely in place."

We definitely want to make sure they are safely secured in place, Ben thought. "You've got lots of stanchions and heavy chains, so I can guarantee that when we are finished this load of crates stay put in heavy seas. We'll also use some of that lumber to make a crib around the crates on either side. Wedge them securely in place as well."

The loading foreman said to Ben, "We've also got spare tarpaulins that I want you to use to cover all them crates as best as you can. I know that the crates are wrapped in rubber and canvas but those tarpaulins will add another layer of protection for the cargo from any rough seas we might encounter. But I have to tell you, I'll be glad when we are able to unload this ship in England."

"Don't worry, mate. Unless you run into a hurricane, and there are none forecast, you won't have a problem with this load."

"What about a U-boat?" volunteered the foreman with a whimsical nod.

"Pray you don't run into one of those," Ben answers. *My God*, he thought, *little chance of that. You won't be at sea long enough to worry about U-boats. I just hope you get rescued before the entire ship sinks.*

41

5 October 1916. Halifax.

"MY GOD, SANDY, WHAT A GORGEOUS DAY!" HARRY SAID AS he grabbed a steaming cup of Orange Pekoe tea that Sandy had just made.

"As I have always said, Harry, autumn is always the best season in Nova Scotia. The weather's still warm and the air is fresh and crisp. Much better than that shitty weather we usually get in March."

"Agreed. And the colours. Liz and I always take a trip up to the Annapolis Valley before the end of the month. Just the two of us. There is a little inn we stay at. We leave Milly with her grandparents and we just have a romantic weekend. Does a world of good, Sandy."

"I believe you! I could do with a little refresher course in romance right about now."

Harry stretched, put both arms across his knees and said wearily, "I've been thinking about our little project. You know, Mike's idea to find out if there any German saboteurs out there planning any hanky-panky. I'm beginning to think it's a waste of time."

"I agree, Harry. We don't have a lot. Let's see what we actually do have before we abandon the project. As you keep saying, the devil is in the details. What have we got?"

"Let's start with known facts, Sandy. That will be the first column on our chart. "First of all, there are the two ships that exploded in two convoys that left Halifax in the last two months. Unexplained explosions. Just like all those ships blowing up after leaving New York."

Sandy added, "Both explosions unexplained. No U-boats or collisions with other boats. No icebergs."

"So. What are the similarities between the explosions?"

"Both ships left Halifax in convoys heading to England." Both took on freight in Halifax, I believe. I'll verify that."

"While you're at it, might as well find out the names of the stevedore crews that were on those loading parties. Next column on our chart should be suspects. Do we have any other suspicious things happening other than these two boats, Sandy?"

"Far as I can tell, just gossip. Things like people overhearing someone wanting to blow up the submarine nets. Or rumours about hearing German bombers on their way to bomb Halifax. And people being on the lookout for suspicious characters."

"So, no real suspects and no other incidents. We have two persons of interest, but they're not suspected of anything. Just Packy's gut feeling. Let's leave it at that. When you gather all the information about the two ships let's meet again and see what we have, Sandy."

"OK by me."

42

6 October 1916. Halifax.

THE NOON GUN ON CITADEL HILL HAD JUST GONE OFF when Harry bolted out of his office chair, flung both arms up as far as they would go and let out a giant gasp of air. A startled officer looked up from across the large room. "Sorry Dan, I didn't mean to frighten you. My back was so stiff from poring over this paperwork, I just had to stretch a bit to relieve the pain. Think I need to go into the back room and have a bite to eat."

As he headed towards the back room the front desk sergeant called out to Harry, "A minute, Harry. I've got an old friend of yours here. Says he wants to have a quick word."

"Packy. What are you doing here? Not in any trouble I hope?"

Packy sported a lopsided grin. *More of a cross between a smile and a smirk*, Harry thought as he gave Packy a warm handshake.

"I've some new information, Harry. Not evidence like you were looking for, but maybe a bit more than gossip. Maybe I should come back later. I'd hate to spoil your meal break."

"Tell you what. I don't have enough time to go out with you, but I would like to invite you to sit with me in the back room. Liz has made me two large sandwiches, more than I can eat. We'll share them and I'll make a fresh pot of tea. And we can talk."

"I hate to be a nuisance, Harry. That's why I waited until today to talk to you. Rita told me I should tell you, just in case it might be important."

Harry led Packy up the three short steps from the reception area to the hallway leading to the back room. "Take a seat, Packy." Harry filled a pot with water and placed it on the small stove to heat up. He added a piece of kindling for good measure to heat the stove a bit. He found a couple of saucers and gave Packy half an egg and half a ham sandwich. "Tea will take a few minutes. What have you got for me?"

"Last Sunday afternoon me and Rita took a break from our routine and went up to Citadel Hill to visit the old fort museum. It was such a gorgeous day, we decided to follow the path around the hill and head down to the Public Gardens.

"As we came around the bend looking out at the South End, we came across these two guys standing in a little hollow, looking out to the harbour. There wasn't much activity on the water. Just one lonely boat sailing past George's Island. Heading in to the Basin.

One of the guys, the taller one, turned sideways just then and I could see he was watching the boat with a pair of binoculars. Next to him was our red-haired man, Danny. Remember him, Harry? They had a brief conversation and seemed more interested in that than paying any attention to me and Rita. Danny may have glanced our way, but he didn't show any interest. We quickened our pace and were soon out of their sight."

"Huh. That's interesting, "Harry said. "But as you mentioned, interesting but not evidence. I'll add it to our file as background for any future significance. And, Packy, I reiterate—I always appreciate any information you provide."

"I stalled telling you right away because it didn't seem all that important. I was hashing it over with Rita last night, and she mentioned one significant fact that had completely slipped my mind."

"What's that?"

"The ship was flying a red flag. You know, the red flag that is required to be flown on all ships entering the harbour with ammunition aboard."

43

7 October 1916. North Atlantic.

THE CONVOY THAT LEFT HALIFAX EARLY ON WEDNESDAY morning was preparing for its fourth day at sea. The weather had been calm when the convoy had departed Halifax, but they encountered very strong winds late on Thursday that persisted throughout the night until noontime on Friday. There were fifteen crew manning the HMS *Justica*, and most would tell you they preferred a bit of rough weather if it meant bad hunting for U-boats.

There were twenty ships in the convoy, which maintained an average speed of 15 knots. The HMS *Justica* was stationed near the rear of the convoy, in close proximity to a British destroyer, which the *Justica* crew felt provided a bit of protective cover for the ammunition ship. After all, if a German U-boat was going to launch a torpedo aimed at the *Justica* it would be blocked by the destroyer. Wouldn't it? Maybe that was just wishful thinking, but it did help push a sailor's fear a little back further in his mind.

All through the night until the wind abruptly died on Friday, crew members carried out their duties in a more careful manner than when the seas were calm. A total inspection of the ship took place on Friday afternoon, and only minor damage had occurred. A vital rope securing one of the life boats had come undone. That allowed for a large rip in the life boat's protective canvas. As a result, the life boat had taken in several feet of water.

An inspection was carefully made to the ammunition crates lashed to the bow. They were all intact, just as they had been installed. The red flag that was required to be flown while the ship was in port had been taken down as soon as they had left Halifax, so there was no advertisement to prowling U-boats that this ship contained a cargo of ammunition.

The crew relaxed a bit with calming seas, and though the threat of the lurking German menace was on everyone's mind they felt safe in the news that no U-boats had been sighted anywhere on their remaining route towards England. Only once did someone chuckle, "I didn't see no albatrosses yet." An attempt at humour that betrayed the underlying superstitions held by every sailor since the beginning of sailing.

Long before the crack of dawn the cooks started their breakfast routines. The usual clang of pots and pans was in full swing when a loud explosion shattered the still sleeping crew. The night-watch officer was just scanning his surrounding ships when a fireball rose higher than the bridge where he was standing.

Klaxons pierced the stale air of tight sleeping quarters, rousing groggy crew members to sudden alertness and a mad scramble to battle stations. Oily, wet smoke blew into open vents and portholes with hurricane force. The entire prow area of the ship was engulfed in raging flames, about twenty feet high against the slowly creeping sunrise colours.

Nearby ships started their practiced drills for aiding a stricken ship. The port destroyer was ablaze with searchlights, frantically scanning the surrounding water for attacking U-boats. As it darted to and fro it gave the impression of an anxious parent intent on protecting its helpless child. Or an enraged bear standing guard against a threat to her cubs.

As the fire roared, the captain knew all too well that once the fire reached the cargo hold, the ship was doomed. Once that happened, the entire ship would become a giant fireball. He hesitated only a minute to confer with his first mate and immediately issued the command to abandon ship.

Life boats were jettisoned and life vests were hurriedly donned. Nearby ships joined the rescue operation with their own flotilla of life boats. There was a general anxiety to not only board a life boat, but to get as far away as possible from the dreaded explosion they all knew would soon take place. True to tradition, the captain was the last to leave the fated ship.

The explosion, when it came, was spectacular. The fireball was enormous, and spewed out a heat wave that could be felt by everyone in the life boats. To a man, they believed they had been torpedoed by a U-boat, but no one seemed to wonder why the first explosion was on deck high above the waterline, where a torpedo would not reach.

44

8 October 1916. Halifax.

IT WAS A WINDY DAY. HARRY, LIZ AND MADDY HAD TO lean in hard against strong gusts as they made their way out of the main entrance of St. Mary's Cathedral. The ten o'clock mass had just finished. It wasn't all that cold, but they had to hold onto their hats as they made their way along Barrington Street past the Old Burying Ground. Harry always thought it was ironic that the oldest cemetery in Halifax was turned over in 1793 to St. Paul's Anglican Church. And here it was now, directly across the street from the city's main Catholic stronghold.

It took them twenty minutes to reach the Baldwin family home on South Street. It may not have been as grand a house as the mansions on Young Street, but it *was* in the South End, and its grandeur had endured from the Victorian era, when it was built.

The house was three stories, with an enormous bay window looking east over the harbour. A large maple dining table, able to seat twelve, held center stage here. Directly behind and facing a large backyard of trees was the parlour, with its large fireplace, bookshelves and six-foot paned windows.

Margaret Baldwin was waiting with the front door open as Liz and Milly made their way up the stone steps. She gave a kiss to Liz and a big hug to Milly. And a smaller hug to Harry." Give me your coats and go sit in front of that warm fire. You must be frozen. Peter will be here in a little while. Madeline is working a day shift at the Infirmary, so it will just be us for Sunday dinner."

Liz looked at her mother, "And Dad, where is he?"

"Over at the mayor's house." Francis Martin was the mayor of Halifax and had been a close friend of Donald's since childhood. He lived only two blocks away. "Frank sent his youngest son over to ask your father to come for a quick chat. Said it couldn't wait."

Just at that moment, Donald arrived and slowly mounted the front steps. "Good morning, Harry," he said with a panting voice. Harry held the door for him as the leprechaun made his way into the hallway. Harry often entertained an amusing image of Donald as a leprechaun. Although Donald didn't have a mane of curly red hair, he did have a lot of curly white hair and a full white mustache that flared like bristles on either side of his rosy red nose. Round red cheeks and a perpetually smiling mouth completed the illusion.

"I've just come from Frank's house. He has some news that I think you'll be interested in hearing." Donald put his hand on Harry's shoulder and ushered him into the back parlour.

"Something you heard from the mayor?" Harry suggested.

"Maybe you didn't pay much attention to it, but a convoy left Halifax on Wednesday heading for England."

"Indeed, I do remember that," Harry was quick to reply. He seemed a bit miffed that Donald might think he wasn't paying attention to his duties and looking for German saboteurs.

"Don't tie your knickers in a knot, son, I'm just saying the news I have just received concerns that convoy. One of the ships, the one laden with ammunition, blew up off the coast of Greenland early yesterday morning. No crew members lost, thank heaven."

"Dad. Harry." Peter stuck his head into the parlour. "I just got here and heard the tail end of your discussion. Mind if I join you?"

"I was just telling Harry that one of the convoy ships that left Halifax on Wednesday blew up early yesterday morning. The ship loaded with explosives."

Harry said with a vehement voice, "That's the third one this year!"

"What've you heard?" said Peter.

"Do you know the name of the ship, Donald?" Harry sensed he was going to be busy with the spy investigation in the coming weeks. There was the slightest bit of excitement in his voice, as if he was already in the throes of building a case.

"It was the HMS *Justica* out of Portsmouth, I believe. It had come to Halifax directly from New York. It was already loaded with ammunition, but it had orders to pick up additional cargo here in Halifax before joining the convoy that left here last Wednesday."

"Causalities?" Harry ventured.

"All safe and accounted for."

"Well, at least the crew were all saved," Peter offered.

Harry sighed, "I've got an itch to find out if we have saboteurs working right here in Halifax. The captain has assigned Sandy and me to begin a secret investigation into German agents working here in Halifax. It's not that it's 'secret secret,' it just has a low priority in our daily police work."

"I'll pray for you."

"Thanks, Peter, but we'll need more than prayers."

"Now Harry, Peter is just trying to be supportive," Donald said. "If our mayor is getting more concerned, then this investigation of yours might gain more traction. But right now, I think we should join the ladies for a nice meal and leave this war talk for another time."

45

9 October 1916. Halifax.

HARRY AND SANDY WERE SEATED IN THE CAPTAIN'S office. Captain Mike Gallagher peered at them with stern eyes. He was not his jovial self on this somber Monday morning.

"The mayor called me on Sunday morning before I even had time to brush my teeth. He wants us to upgrade our German saboteur investigation to more urgent. He wants some action. More research, guys."

"So! It's getting political now."

"That it is, Harry." Mike looked at him with buggy eyes. "That. It. Is."

"Then I guess we'd better pick up our pace. We know there have been three ships sunk on convoys leaving Halifax since the middle of August. One a month. We have to make sure there won't be another one next month."

Mike interjected, "All well and good, Harry, but without some clear thinking it's kind of hard to prepare for the unknown. We need some facts to focus our attention."

Sandy raised his hand. "From what I understand, all three ships took on supplies in Halifax. None of the ships anchored in the Basin were ever touched."

"As far as we know," added Harry. "I do have a piece of information to share with the both of you. Information that I received on Friday afternoon that suddenly seems more important than it did on Friday."

"Let's have it."

Harry took a deep breath. And a big gulp of tea. "You guys both know Packy O'Leary. He's part of the landscape of Sailor Town. He's a decent sort, friendly and all that. He sometimes hears things that he thinks might interest me. Mostly rumours, but occasionally there's a nugget of useful information."

Mike slapped the table, "I remember that time Packy told you about that scumbag he kept running into over at the Pig. Seems this guy was from a small town in New Brunswick. He almost killed a bloke who was messing around with his wife, even though the wife had left him after years of abuse. It was Packy's hearsay evidence that put you on the trail of that guy."

"And Sandy." Harry reminded him. "Sandy and I both ended up arresting him for attempted murder. That story reinforces my point that Packy hangs out in scuzzy places where people drink too much and sometimes say things they wouldn't say if they were sober. Not that the Pig is a scuzzy place, mind you.

"Anyway, back in May, Packy told me he overheard some suspicions characters talking about blowing up the submarine nets. Nothing came of that. Later he told me he saw one of those same characters at Rita's. He even identified him as an Irishman named Danny Sullivan. Said his curly red hair stood out like a tattoo. I thanked Packy for the information, told him to keep his eyes open, but please don't call me every time you hear a rumour. I guess that's why he waited a week before he got in touch with me."

Mike stood up and stretched his stiff back. He leaned on the back of his chair, "I understand perfectly what you're saying. Tell us about the report."

"A week ago, Saturday, Packy and Rita were visiting the old fort up on Citadel Hill, enjoying a leisurely autumn day. As they were rounding the hill from the fort entrance, they saw two men standing in a little dip below them. The taller of the two was looking through his binoculars at a ship moving up the harbour towards the Basin. Packy could see that the ship was flying a red flag. He recognized the shorter guy right away, Danny Sullivan. He grabbed Rita and they hightailed it out of sight before they were seen."

"And he waited a week to tell you?" said Sandy.

"For the reason I have stated. It was late on Friday and I was just heading home. When I heard the news of the exploding ship on Sunday, all the bits of the jigsaw fell into place. Danny Sullivan and his friend were tracking the course of the HMS *Justica*."

46

10 October 1916. Halifax.

IT WAS EXACTLY TEN O'CLOCK WHEN HARRY ARRIVED AT the Waterfront Security Commission offices. Harry wore his best blue suit, a crisp, white shirt and a dark red tie knotted tightly in place. Just like he expected the ex-military man to dress for their meeting.

Liz had helped with the knot and said he looked *so handsome*. She gave him a nice embrace and a peck on the cheek before sending him on his way.

The commission offices were located on the top floor of an old brick building that had been built back in the 1880's but was still a solid and much used structure. Warren Smith's office commanded a panoramic view of the harbour and provided a vantage point to view all shipping traffic passing into and out of Bedford Basin.

"Good morning, Detective and welcome to my abode." Warren greeted him with a hearty handshake. Firm and dry. Just like the last time. Same impeccable grooming and military erectness.

"It's Harry. Remember our first introduction? We're on a first name basis.

"Roger that."

"It's only been a little over a month since we met, and now we've had another ship exploding at sea after leaving Halifax."

"Yep. Third one since August."

"That's true, Warren. We've started a low-key investigation to find out if there's any evidence that there were German saboteurs working in Halifax. We didn't find any evidence, but came up with some suspicions. Like a bad smell blowing in the wind. We don't know the source of the smell, but we know it's there."

"Like the smell that greets you when you enter a home where a turkey is cooking."

"Yeah, like that. But that's a good smell. What we are smelling is a stink that needs to be tracked back to its source."

"How can I help you, Harry?"

"Since this latest sinking our investigation is being ramped up, and we are going to allot more energy and resources to determine if there is indeed a conspiracy here. First, I would like to revisit our investigation with you regarding the *Port of Dover*.

"The coal carrier."

"The night watchman died of a broken neck caused by a fall from the upper deck. There were no bruises or marks on the body to indicate a struggle before he fell. No evidence of foul play. There's no physical evidence to support any theory that the night watchman, Chesley Smith, was pushed to his death."

"That was in the coroner's report, Harry."

"My wife says I have a suspicious mind. She says that's a good quality for a man in my line of work. First, Chesley was partway through his evening meal. He had a half a cup of tea sitting on his desk, along with a half-eaten sandwich. Something startled him, because he dropped his sandwich on the table and went to look out over the hold. That's where he fell. If he had simply got up to go to the head, he would probably have finished his meal first. No, I believe he was startled and then ambushed and pushed over the rail to his death."

"Maybe, Harry. Why would someone do that? Do you think there was a motive?"

"The motive. That's easy. Someone wanted to plant a bomb in the empty hold, and they could only do that by eliminating the only witness around. They knew that the hold would be filled with coal and would conceal any bombs they planted."

"Well, I can see that your logic is sound. At least, it makes sense to me."

"What I need from you, Warren, is a list of the stevedore crew members who were assigned to each of the three ships that took on supplies in Halifax. See if there's any commonality there. That's my starting point."

"I'd be glad to help. Should be able to get that list by Friday at the latest. I can tell you one thing, though. The crew that loaded coal onto the *Port of Dover* would have been a specialty crew. They're all trimmers with experience working in coal mines. A dirty job, Harry. The ship would have been moved over to the coal jetty for them to do the loading. There are a lot of different compartments in the hold. It's important that all the loose coal be properly secured, because a rough sea could shift the coal in such a way that it might cause an unstable ballast problem."

"Like the other ships, this crew would have had direct access to the hold. So, make sure you include them. One last thing, Warren. And I don't want to put you on the spot. But if you've any suspicions about anyone—someone bad-mouthing Americans or Brits, or showing some kind of sympathy for Germany—please let me know. On the QT. Between you and me."

"I'll certainly do that, Harry. Now, do you want to go over to the pier and look at the shed where the cargo for the *Justica* was being stored? Pier 15 is just a short walk."

Warren pulled on his navy-blue jacket and joined Harry for

the walk. The two of them could easily have been mistaken for military men or bankers from the Bank of Nova Scotia, although Harry still had the aura of a cop about him.

"When the HMS *Justica* arrived in Halifax, it was flying the red flag required of all ships carrying a cargo of ammunition or any other explosive materials. It's meant as a warning to all other ships to be careful when encountering that ship in Halifax's very busy and very narrow harbour. It also acts as a beacon identifying a target for any would-be saboteur."

"Agreed. I also know that there was a secret consignment of TNT arranged by the Canadian Government that had to be loaded onto the *Justica*, a secret only a few people knew."

"That's already part of my own investigation, Harry. Finding out who was privy to that information. Any saboteurs would've known about this consignment beforehand if they were going to tamper with it. The main cargo was already loaded in New York, and the cargo hold was sealed."

"Which meant that no stevedore would have any access to the hold."

"Exactly. There were sixteen crates of TNT on eight pallets. The crates themselves were each encased in heavy, rubbery plastic to keep the cargo dry and prevent the crates from knocking together in heavy seas. They were also covered in canvas. Each crate was examined for any tampering. The pallets were loaded on the deck of the *Justica* and lashed tightly and securely in place and draped with tarpaulins. It would have taken a cyclone to dislodge them."

They reached the corrugated shed, which looked like an unlikely place to store valuable cargo. Harry voiced this to Warren. You call this a secure location for storing ammunition?"

"We took comfort in the fact that it was such an insignificant shed in a little-used area of a messy dock that no one would even suspect something of value would be stored here. The shed itself was only used for storing broken pallets and other useless junk that should have been thrown out except that nobody bothered to do it. It was thought to be the perfect hiding place, because it didn't arouse anybody's interest."

"Did you know, Warren, that Sherlock Holmes came across a similar scene in one of his cases? He used the term *hiding in plain sight* to describe the hiding place. That sure fits here."

They were met at the shed by Bernie Frost, who was waiting for them. "Bernie, I'd like you to meet detective Harry Frobisher. Harry, Bernie was the foreman for the stevedore crew that loaded those TNT boxes onto the *Justica*."

"Good day, Bernie. Please, call me Harry. I'd like to ask you a few questions about the day you loaded that cargo. Can you tell me what you remember?"

"Be glad to, but I don't think I have anything to add to what I've already told Warren's people. That ship, the *Justica,* was late arriving and didn't get here until after the noon gun. We had a crew of four twiddling their thumbs with nothing to do."

"You also had an inspector on site to supervise the loading, correct?

"We had two inspectors, one from the military, and the agent from ship's owners."

"Do you remember the names of the stevedores who worked that day?"

"They were all familiar faces. I knew some them by their first name. Bob and Frank, for instance."

"Warren here is going to make a list for me of all the men that worked that day. If you have any comments to make, please tell Warren. Odd behaviour, anything suspicious. Anything that seems unusual."

"I can't think of anything like that, but now that you've jogged my memory, there was one little incident. The shed was padlocked, and I had brought the keys with me. Went I went to open the lock the keys didn't fit. I heard someone snicker, which pissed me off. So, I used a crowbar to rip off the damn lock."

"And everything looked intact inside the shed?"

"Right as rain."

"And the loading went smoothly?"

"As far as I was concerned. And I also felt reassured because the agent, Mr. Barr, spent a lot of time inspecting the cargo. Making sure it was well secured and covered because, you know, it was all stored on the open deck."

"Thank you, Bernie, and thank you, Warren. I've got what I need for the time being, and now I have to get back to the station. If you can get that list to me by Friday, Warren, I would appreciate it."

47

29 November 1917. New York.

BY TUESDAY MORNING ALL THE HOLDS OF THE *MONT Blanc* had been sealed, and stevedores began loading the benzol. Benzol was high-octane gasoline and was stored in iron drums, but remained highly volatile. Even though the drums were tightly sealed the smell of gasoline was as pervasive as any commercial gas station. The morning breeze was a welcome guest that carried most of the smell away from the ship.

Captain Aimé Le Médec and First Officer Jean Glotin were huddled together in the wheelhouse, peering down at the activity going on below them. The captain finished the last dregs of his coffee and banged his cup into its holding cage with a little more force than was necessary. "It's one thing to volunteer for hazardous duty, Jean, but it's altogether another matter to have it forced upon you, especially in such a sneaky way as our agent has done."

Jean thought to himself, *Fuck you, Flowers*, and he knew in his heart that Aimé felt the same way but would never say so out loud.

"I'm as angry as you, Aimé, but we've been over this so often that we have no choice now but to finish this mission and pray we don't have an accident or get torpedoed by a German U-boat. Meanwhile, I've lectured the crew to be extra cautious in lashing those barrels to the deck. Make them so secure that a violent storm at sea cannot dislodge them. I've also instituted a total ban on any matches on deck, and limited smoking to a very few areas."

"You're a good man, Jean, and I'm proud to be working with you."

"We've got a good crew for support as well. They weren't happy with having their smoking curtailed, but they gave a rousing cheer of support when I issued the orders and they said they would take up chewing tobacco instead."

During the next three days the stevedores and crew members loaded over fifty barrels of highly flammable Benzol. There was a lot of open cargo space fore and aft of the main cabin area, including the open space on the rear deck that jutted out over the rudder. Every barrel was lashed tightly to the railing and any other post that acted as a support. Every precaution was taken to guard against lethal risks to the ship and crew.

Those risks ranged from violent storms at sea to something as simple as nudging a dock too hard. Anything that could dislodge those barrels on deck. An attack by a German U-boat was the most worrisome weight. It was a cloud that hung over the thoughts of the 39 merchant seamen who had signed up for this mission. For this suicide mission.

Le Médec and Glotin had moved out onto deck and were leaning over the starboard railing. "What worries me most of all, Jean, is all that TNT in hold number two. If it explodes, not a man aboard this ship would survive. The *Mont Blanc* is a floating bomb."

48

20 October 1916. Halifax.

BEN STENDT MIGHT HAVE HAD A GERMAN NAME, BUT SO did a lot of other people in Halifax and throughout Nova Scotia. Most had been here since the late 1800s. Their children were born in Canada, so many of them were automatically bona fide Canadian citizens. Although Ben had not been born in Canada, he was a Canadian citizen and had lived in Halifax long enough to be accepted as a Haligonian.

He was recognized as a hard worker and was accepted as a no-nonsense kind of guy. He wasn't warm and friendly, and didn't seem to have any close friends, but you could count on him to get the job done. Which was why he was most often picked as the supervisor for the stevedore gangs he worked with on the waterfront. Nobody could understand why he seemed to befriend Danny Sullivan, a complainer and slacker whom most of the men barely tolerated.

This Friday had been busier than normal. Everyone who could work was called in that day. Ben and his crew, which included Danny Sullivan, were knackered after their shift finished at 5 PM, and it didn't take much effort for the thirstier ones to steer the crew to the Pigs Revenge.

They started out with ongoing complaints about the day's work load and how unfair life was. Then the topic of conversation turned to women and sex, as it always did. Finally, the old war grudges were brought out, and tempers began to simmer. By seven o'clock, most of the family men had left. Danny and the remaining few were into their cups. No one seemed to notice that Ben was still on his first round.

"Come on Danny, let's sit over in the corner. I'll buy you a meal. I need to discuss something with you in private. Besides, I can see that these guys are beginning to annoy you." With that he took a firm grip on Danny's elbow and led him over to a far corner of the room.

"You OK, Danny? Staying out of trouble?"

Danny let out a big spew of smoke. "I'm OK Long as I got something to drink and a bit of tail now and again. Work's been steady. Keeping me busy."

"And out of trouble, I hope. Do you still go over to Harriet's?"

"Often enough. You might say I'm a bit of a regular."

"I suppose that's good, Danny. Long as you don't go off the deep end and start spouting off about how the Irish wouldn't mind if Germany prevailed in the war against England."

"It's not that I'm a fan of the Kaiser, it's just that I wouldn't mind if England loses the war. I don't think you would see many Irish shed tears if that were to happen."

"Have you heard any rumours about a police investigation into the sinking of those three ships that exploded after leaving Halifax?"

"Nobody has asked me anything. But I did hear some talk that the police do have some interest in those ships. Seems they have asked for a list of all the men who worked on the three crews."

"I've heard those rumours too. But I haven't heard that the police are asking about anybody in particular. What I need you to do, Danny is keep your ears open, especially in taverns and those houses of ill repute you frequent. As you know, people often say things they shouldn't say when they've had too much to drink. See if you can find out who is asking questions and what they are asking about. But for God's sake, be discrete. We don't want to draw any attention to ourselves."

"Are we going to be doing another job anytime soon?"

"My contact in New York promised me a new supply back in September, but so far nothing has arrived. My contact was also a little anxious. He had a suspicion he was being followed. Ever since the Black Tom explosion there've been a lot of police nosing around New York. So, he might not be able to send us anything. We do, however, have enough for one more attempt."

"Anything in particular"

"No. But I want you to be very careful about what you say and do. Don't create any reasons to draw police attention to yourself."

49

31 January 1917. Halifax.

ON 28 DECEMBER, PAUL KOEING WAS ARRESTED IN NEW
Jersey for conducting sabotage against the U.S. government. As if
in response, beginning in the new year there was a spate of bombings in the United States, both on land and at sea. Between 10
and 15 January, three DuPont plants that manufactured explosive
powder suffered heavy damage from serious fires. Later in the
month, two British ships, the SS *Sygna* and SS *Ryndam*, exploded
at sea. Two undetonated bombs were found on the SS *Rosebank*
before it set sail.

Ben still had his remaining stash of ten cigar bombs, which he
had carefully hidden in a well concealed niche in his basement.
Because he had been subjected to heavy-duty surveillance since
the summer, Koeing had never managed to send Ben the supplies
he had promised back in September.

The United States had greatly increased security around waterfront loading areas, and some of this effort had spilled over into
Halifax. There had been no opportunities for Ben to plant any
further bombs since the HMS *Justica* back in October. And with
the rash of bombings in New York this past month, security had
been increased even more, with random body searches of dock
workers who loaded war cargos on ships heading out in convoys.

Captain Mike Gallagher had set up a meeting with Harry and

Sandy to review the status of their investigation and to determine its ongoing mission. There had been no suspicious activity on the waterfront and no ship explosions since the loss of the HMS *Justica*.

It had been snowing since midnight, and the streets were clogged with snow banks. By noon the snow had petered out, but the wind was still howling in strong gusts as it rounded over Citadel Hill. It was not a good day to be out and about. *A good day to have long overdue meeting on our investigation*, thought Mike.

Harry wiped a spot clean on one of the small paned windows overlooking the harbour. All he saw was whiteout. "Brrr" is what he exclaimed. Not that he was cold in the overheated police station, but he was reflecting on his chilling trudge from the Olde English restaurant. "I brought you two a treat. Fresh blueberry muffins baked by Brenda herself."

"And I've just brewed up a big pot of tea. So, let's have a snack before we get into it," offered Sandy.

Captain Gallagher laid a pile of folders on the larger conference table. "A snowy day like this is usually a quiet day for the police department. I thought we could use the quiet time to take a good, hard look at our German agent search." He pushed the blackboard into place so that the three of them could easily access it. "And I really do appreciate your attendance in spite of the weather."

Harry wiped some crumbs from his shirt. "Sandy has done most of the leg work and he's organized all of the research, so why don't you start off, Sandy?"

"If you look at this blackboard, I have drawn up some timelines showing known facts and when they happened. There are three sets of dates referring to the three ships that exploded after leaving Halifax in convoys headed to England. These dates refer to the arrival and departure times, as well as the dates the explosions occurred."

Sandy took a drink of tea and continued. "With the help of Warren Smith and his staff, we also have a list of the stevedores who worked on the crews servicing those three ships. From that list we've identified only two stevedores who worked on all three ships: Ben Stendt and Daniel Sullivan."

Harry interjected, "Mike, we are presenting you not only with facts, but hopefully also with evidence, which is what we are all looking for. Also, we're including circumstantial evidence, hunches, plausible explanations, even 'what ifs,' which can't be used in court but might lead us to evidence. To quote Sherlock Holmes: 'When you eliminate all the known facts of a case, what you have left is most often the truth.' That's our guiding light."

"To continue, Mike," said Sandy, "there's one slight problem to begin with. The crew that was assigned to the *Port of Dover*, the coal carrier, didn't actually load anything. They weren't needed and were never on board the ship. But they were aware that the ship was tied up at the dry dock for repairs, with no supervision except an old night watchman. For that reason, we are keeping the same two stevedores on the lists of all three ships."

"All right, do we have anybody else at all that we might be interested in?" Mike said in his loud baritone voice.

Harry replied, "There are always so many rumours, as you know, Mike. People have a grudge against their neighbor and before you know it the neighbor is a German spy. We try and keep an eye on our German population in an unintrusive way, but all of the reports we investigate about them are driven by prejudice, pure and simple. And of course, there's all the drivel that catches hold of people after they've spent a night drinking at the Pig."

"Like Packy, you mean?"

"Packy comes from a good family and still lives with his mother. He's got a good education, and it's a crying shame he's saddled with an alcohol addiction. I trust him, and with some coaxing he has learned not to come to me with every single rumour he hears. However, some of his information is keeping me alerted to the two main characters we're interested in."

"The two stevedores," piped in Sandy. "And don't forget, Mike, it was Packy's hearsay evidence that he picked up at the Pig that led us to that guy we arrested from New Brunswick. The one who tried to murder his wife."

Harry continued, "Packy first noticed those two in the Pig's Revenge. They just seemed to Packy's sneaky disposition like two guys huddled together to plan a nefarious deed. Like blowing up the submarine nets. Then there was an incident up at Harriet's. The Irish guy, Danny Sullivan, got into a row with some American merchantmen. It was loud and became very boisterous. When the fisticuffs started Harriet called the cops.

"Packy wasn't there but Rita was. Rita and Packy have an intimate relationship, and she often tells him about gossip that's picked up in her parlour. With Packy's vivid description of Sullivan's curly red hair and surly disposition, Rita figured that that was who her customer was. In fact, it was Rita who provided us with the Irishman's name.

"To continue, Sullivan had been ranting about the war. He was telling people that he had no love for the Kaiser but wished that Germany would conquer England. And then he started haranguing the two Americans for providing England with war supplies when they were supposed to be a neutral country. That's when things got out of hand."

"You've got to admit it, Mike," Sandy jumped in, "it does give Sullivan a motive."

"There's more," Harry continued. "On that day back in September when the HMS *Justica* arrived in Halifax harbour, Packy and Rita had been visiting the fort up on Citadel Hill. They caught sight of two guys paying attention to the harbour traffic. One guy had bright red, curly hair. The other guy was tall and lean. The tall guy had a pair of binoculars and seemed intent on following the progress of a ship in the harbour flying a red flag. Rita and Packy high-tailed it out of there. They were sure they hadn't been seen, but you never know."

Mike cleared his throat. "Let me summarize what we have so far. Fact: the list of ships, dates, etc. Fact: the lists of the crews, which we can mate with the list of ships." Circumstantial evidence. These two guys worked on all the ships that exploded. Both were seen watching the HMS *Justica* sail up Halifax harbour. The Irishman ranted about how much he hated England. Which I suppose also gives him a motive. Where do we go from here?"

Harry knew that making assumptions could lead you down a rabbit hole. He knew that trying to prove that someone was guilty and looking for facts to support that guilt was a sure way of missing out on evidence pointing to different conclusions. "We should keep our eyes open and look for any evidence that there might be other German agents active in Halifax. We have to keep an open mind that there might be, otherwise it restricts our focus to only two people."

"I agree, Harry," Mike replied, "but what do we do about our only suspects?"

Harry explained his plan. "If it is indeed them, and in my gut, I do feel it's them, we have to keep a watchful eye on them. Maybe they'll make a mistake. I think we should alert our border control services to keep a lookout as well and report any suspicious travel to the United States. And, we should keep our files up to date with any rumours or actual suspicious events that come our way about these two."

Sandy's voice was tinged with frustration. "It's been over three months now since the HMS *Justica* went down. Waterfront security has been tight. A lot of that has been a spillover from the United States, where police and secret service agents have ratcheted up their surveillance of enemy agents." Sandy swallowed. "I think, (a) there haven't been any opportunities, or (b) they have run out of bombs. Not only has the American supply of bombs dwindled, bringing them into Canada is a lot harder now. Not much else we can do but wait and keep alert to suspicious activity."

50

14 February 1917. Halifax.

VALENTINE'S DAY.

Harry was feeling good. Romance was in his heart as he bounded into the police station. "Sandy, I'm in love."

"Does your wife know about this, Harry?"

"Funny man. Tonight, I'm bringing roses home to my lovely wife, and I've reserved a table at the Lord Nelson Hotel."

"Good for you, Harry. I'm buying roses for my wife, too, but I think we are having meatloaf for dinner."

"I hope nothing major happens today. I'd love to leave early."

Nothing happened for an hour and a half. At 10:30 a young man arrived out of breath with a look of high anxiety on his face. He was ushered into the captain's office, from whence a loud voice bellowed five minutes later for Harry and Sandy to drop everything and join the young man.

"Gentlemen, this is Stan Forbes from Imperial Oil. He has just come across the harbour on the Dartmouth ferry. He came to this station from Imperoyl in a panic, and I think we need to act on his information immediately. Mr. Forbes, please tell Harry and Sandy what you just told me."

"I work at the new Imperoyl Refinery they're building over on the site of old Fort Clarence. We're building new crude oil storage tanks urgently needed for the war effort. Three tanks are already finished and filled to capacity. I'm the assistant foreman for the crew building a fourth tank."

Harry interjected, "It's not hard to see those tanks when you look across the harbour towards McNab's Island. I've often wondered if the security there is as high as it should be, when it could well be a target for some German saboteur."

Forbes looked at Harry with bulging eyes. "That's exactly what has happened," he exclaimed. At least, it's what we suspect. One of the crewmen took a break early this morning and went over to a quiet corner by one of the tanks to take a piss. While he was doing his business, he noticed a small canvas bag jammed underneath the tank. Almost as if someone were trying to hide it. He tried to pull it out and loosened the top enough to see a bunch of glass tubes. And to his credit, he knew it was something fishy.

"He brought the foreman over to have a look. The foreman was able to remove one of the tubes, which he brought over to the site manager. The site manager was startled. He had heard about explosive devices called cigar bombs, but he had no idea how they functioned. He didn't know if this was one of those devices, but he wasn't going to take any chances.

"He ordered the tube to be taken out of the office and hidden as far away as possible from any of the storage tanks. There's no telephone at the site office, so he sent me over here to ask for your assistance. He said he was going to order a full evacuation as a precaution."

Harry stared straight into Sandy's face and said with a wide smile, "Sandy, this could be a break for us. If they are indeed the cigar bombs we have been reading about in the news from the United States, and if we could get a hold of one, it would be hard evidence for our investigation. I don't know how stable these things are. And I wouldn't want anybody nearby if one exploded."

Sandy raised his hand and pointed to Harry. "My uncle Jack works over at Artillery Place, which is army headquarters for harbour security. Part of his job is to keep fully informed about possible threats to any vessel using Halifax Harbour and the Basin. He has some good military contacts in New York and is well informed about shipping-related sabotage incidents throughout New England. On top of that, he has one specialist who knows more about these cigar bombs than anyone else in the country."

"Who's that, Sandy?" Mike piped in with some authority. "Can we get hold of him right now? I want him to join us immediately and accompany Harry over to Imperoyl for an assessment."

"His name is Robert Fife, and I've met him personally several times. I wouldn't say he was obsessed with explosives, but he has a strong interest in them and has accumulated a lot of knowledge. A year ago, he spent a week in New Jersey at a training course and has had first-hand exposure to these devices. I'm sure he is at work right now, and as soon as I can get a hold of him, I'll tell him we need him immediately and will send someone to pick him up."

Everyone felt a jolt of enthusiasm as the calvary heeded the call to action. They picked up Robert Fife at Artillery Place and made it to the ferry in record time. Sandy made the introductions. "Harry, I would like you to meet Bob Fife. Bob, this is my partner Harry and this lad here is Stan. He works over at Imperoyl and was on the construction site when the bomb discovery was made this morning." They had a brief meeting with Bob on the rear deck as the ferry coddled them with a smooth crossing to Dartmouth. They disembarked just as the noon gun boomed from Citadel Hill.

There was a car waiting for them. On the trip over Bob had explained how he'd been shown a cigar bomb in New Jersey and had actually handled one. He assured them that if the copper plug in the centre of this tube they found was still thick enough, it would take a couple of hours yet before the sulfuric acid ate its way through the copper disc. The time to detonation depended on how much of the copper plug remained. "Better let me see that tube before I can give you an assessment. If we're lucky and the plug is still in good shape, I could probably disarm those suckers in less than a half hour."

They were met at the construction site by the site manager and the crewman who had found the package. The crewman told them about his experience. "I needed to take a leak, and tried to find a space out of sight of the others. That's why I went up there by the tank. Until I reached that spot, I couldn't see the package. It wasn't visible unless you were on top of it."

The site manager and Bob went alone to inspect the tube where it been hidden in a safe shelter behind some large rocks. Bob picked it up, had a good look and replaced it where it lay. They returned to the others.

"Do you believe in good luck, fellows?" Bob asked.

"More than I do in prayer," exhaled Harry. "Can we actually disarm these things?"

Bob rested his hand on Harry's shoulder. "Until that acid in the top part of the tube eats its way through the copper, these things are very safe. Even if you drop one it won't explode. Only if you drop one and the tube cracks, allowing the two liquids to mix, will you have an explosion. Don't forget, those saboteurs have to carry those bombs on their person, sometimes for several hours, before they are able to plant them."

Sandy looked expectantly at Bob, "So, what happens now?"

"I had a good look at the tube. It has been armed, which is as simple as pulling out the tab that keeps the sulfuric acid from eating away at the copper plug. It looks like it can hold out for a good few hours yet. Maybe longer. I just hope the rest of the tubes in that bag have the same size plug.

"What I need is one of your welder's masks, pliers, a knife and a non-metal container that can hold sulfuric acid. The mask is for my protection, although it won't help much if there's an explosion. The task is simple. I remove the top cap from each tube and pour the sulfuric acid into the container. And *voila*, the bomb is disarmed."

Bob looked carefully at the remaining thickness of each copper plug and estimated that there were more than five hours remaining before any of the tubes would have exploded. In less than an hour, he disarmed all the tubes and rinsed them with hot soapy water to cleanse them of any residual sulfuric acid.

"Here's one for you to take back to the office, Harry. It's completely safe. Just be aware that there's picric acid in the lower part of the tube, not water. Keep it in a dry, safe place. I'll take the rest with me."

51

6 April 1917. Washington.

THE UNITED STATES DECLARED WAR ON GERMANY.

Up until this date, the U.S. was officially a neutral country, even though it overtly kept supplying war materials and other war-time necessities to England and France. President Woodrow Wilson had narrowly won re-election the previous year on an anti-war platform, and despite his efforts and the efforts of the German ambassador to avoid war, it was inevitable.

There was widespread sentiment among German Americans for the United States to remain neutral. Added to that, religious groups strongly promoted pacificism. Wilson himself was a devoted Presbyterian and promoted his religious beliefs as a justification to avoid war.

None of these efforts prevailed, and on this day the United States formally declared war against Germany.

American neutrality aside, Germany had stepped up its campaign to disrupt the flow of goods from the United States to its enemies in Europe, especially Great Britain. Starting on 1 February, German submarines were ordered to begin unrestricted warfare against American shipping.

While Germany had touted the idea that the United States could still remain neutral despite shipping losses, this was nothing more than useless posturing. In reality Germany knew the United States was ready to declare war.

Mexico had long been a strong supporter of Germany in the war. Germany was well aware of this and had tried to reach out to Mexico to secure their alliance against the United States in the coming declaration of war. To that end, a memorandum had been prepared by the German government, outlining to Mexican authorities the benefits to be enjoyed by Mexico if they formed an a alliance with Germany against the United States.

The memorandum had been sent as a coded telegram to the German Embassy in Washington for retransmission to Mexico. It had been dispatched on 17 January 1917 by Arthur Zimmermann, a top-level civil servant in the Foreign Office of the German government. History would come to know this document as the Zimmerman Telegram.

The telegram had been intercepted by British Intelligence and quickly shared with the Americans. The content of the telegram included plans for Mexico to "reconquer their lost territory in Texas, New Mexico and Arizona." This telegram had shifted public opinion in the U.S., and was at the forefront of efforts to convince Congress to make a declaration of war.

52

20 April 1917. Halifax.

IT WAS RAINING HARD AS HARRY STOOD UNDER THE porch of the police station. But it was a pleasant, warm rain. It smelled of spring. *April showers bring May flowers*, he rhymed in his head. Except for that horrible war that had now officially come to all of North America, Harry was content with his life. They'd just received confirmation yesterday that Liz was pregnant. He thought, *If there really is a God and he is a God of love this new child of ours will be born into a war-free world.*

Harry took a long, satisfying drag of his cigarette. He had one foot up on the low cement railing and was gazing out across the mist-filled harbour when the station house door opened.

"You look too relaxed to be a cop, Harry." Sandy had just lit his own cigarette as he put his foot on the railing next to Harry. "Ruth and I want to extend our congratulations."

"I appreciate it, Sandy. I'll let Liz know."

There hadn't been any new developments in their saboteur investigation since the discovery of the unexploded bombs at Imperoyl. It was useful to know exactly what they were looking out for. Such a small item, and so easily concealed. And so powerful.

"I've been thinking, about how much things have changed here in our little old port city from a year ago," Harry said. Sandy turned to face him. "The Black Tom explosion in New Jersey. The stepped-up security in the U.S. against German saboteurs, not only trying to plant bombs on convoy ships but also in munitions factories. And of course, our very own bombers. I was wondering what happened to them. No activity since last October. I think it has to do with all that work by that New York policeman, Tunny, bringing together all those uncoordinated efforts to chase down German agents plaguing the waterfronts in New York and New Jersey. I'm guessing that strengthened security has also put a damper on supplying bombs to anyone up here in Halifax."

Sandy arched his back and stood on his tip toes to ease his aching back. "I agree with you. And don't forget about all those German diplomats that've been exposed. That must have hurt any networks that were in place. It must've been a blow for them when the mad bomber fled to Mexico. That surely put a crimp in their bomb supply."

"No doubt about that, Sandy. And with war finally declared it's going to be that much harder to renew a concerted campaign in the U.S. and in Canada. I wonder about that attack against our refinery. My theory is that they haven't had any opportunities to go after any ships, and this refinery was just a soft target."

"I've got to go inside, Harry. Too much tea this morning is taking its toll. One last thought, though. I am sure our boys are still out there. Have faith and be ready for an opportunity. Something's going to happen, I can feel it in my bones. We've just got to be ready when it does happen."

Harry lit another cigarette. It had stopped raining, and the air felt clean and fresh, with no smell of salt at all. Like it had been washed. Sandy's comment reminded him of his conversation with Peter during breakfast with the family last Sunday. Liz had never approved of Harry's contempt for religion. His conversations with her brother often seemed tinged with religious challenges.

Peter's life was the church. He was guided by religious principles, Christian values, faith in God. Too much faith, thought Harry. Peter had said that you were either a believer or not, that faith was the most important ingredient in life. To which Harry had replied with a little too much sarcasm that facts didn't matter a whit to a believer. *It's a good thing my dear Liz quickly put an end to that conversation*, he said to himself.

Maybe religious believers don't need facts, but in my line of work facts are paramount. So are gut instincts, which could be likened to beliefs, I suppose. We've got a few facts about our investigation—unexploded bombs, a dead night watchman—and a hell of a lot of circumstantial evidence. I'm ready to be convinced otherwise, but my gut feeling says those two guys are our culprits. However, this certainty doesn't hold water if there are no facts or evidence to back up my belief. I wish I had power like religions do. Then I could just say, this is the truth, I don't need to prove anything.

Peter lives in a religious world. I prefer the world of Sherlock Holmes.

53

30 April 1917. Halifax.

IT HAD BEEN A SHORT WORKDAY AT THE SHIPYARDS. ONE cargo to load, which was completed by noon. The crew was dismissed shortly thereafter. Not that Ben minded very much. It was a nice warm day, and he decided he didn't want to do anything but enjoy it. Being the solitary man he was, he was quite comfortable with his own company. On the way back to his saltbox he picked up a nice piece of rib eye and some spuds. This will go well with my pickled beets and some cold beer, he thought to himself.

By mid-afternoon he had everything cleaned up and was sitting out on his front step enjoying his fourth beer. And the warm sunshine. From his vantage point he had a direct line of sight to his usual workplace on the waterfront. As he sat there pondering the war now that the Americans were directly involved, he wondered if his sabotage days were over. He only had two cigar bombs left after losing the rest in that fiasco at the refinery. He could only blame himself. Danny had accompanied him during the night, but he was the one who actually armed the bombs and hid them from sight. And they were definitely well hidden, he knew that. Until they got up-close scrutiny from someone needing to empty his bladder in private.

He took another long swig of beer. *I should have used bombs with shorter fuses*, he conceded to himself, *but those were the only ones I had left. Luck. Just bad luck*, he sighed to himself. His main contact in New York, Paul Koeing, had been arrested back in November, and so far, no replacement had tried to get in touch with him. Even though a couple of convoy ships looked like possible opportunities, he had no bomb to plant anyway. Besides, security was so tight he would have to be awfully careful.

As he gazed over the Richmond flats at the Narrows, he swore to himself that if he ever got hold of more bombs, he would find a way to restart his bombing activities. Come hell or high water. Even if that nosey cop kept sniffing around, he would find a way.

54

2 November 1917. New York.

SINCE PAUL KOEING'S ARREST FOR SABOTAGE, HIS NET-work of agents had largely disintegrated over the last year. Despite their constant surveillance of German Embassy officials, Tunny's bomb squad and the Secret Service had difficulty finding any remaining agents. Yet, unbeknownst to the American spy catchers, there was another network of German agents that had been secretly set up by the German Embassy.

Paul Hilken was an American citizen born to German parents. He was a citizen in name only, and he pledged allegiance to Germany first and trusted only those who did the same. He was the heir to the German Lloyd Shipping Company and fiercely loyal to his German roots. He went so far as to insist that his family speak German inside their home.

Hilken was the Baltimore-based paymaster for German spies in the United States, and had been for some time prior to the war. Not only did he work as an agent for Wolf von Igel, the German military attaché, but he also ran a network of spies and saboteurs under the control of Captain Frederick Hinsch.

Captain Hinsch was the ill-tempered skipper of the *Neckar*, a ship of the German Lloyd line, and was Hilken's top enforcer and agent. He was a fierce German committed to helping the Kaiser through intimidation, force and secrecy. By the summer of 1917 he had built up a network of spies and saboteurs that was completely unknown to Tunny and his New York bomb squad.

Also unknown to Tunny and his investigators was Koeing's agent, Frederick Scheindl, who still worked as a clerk at the National City Bank of New York. Maybe it was because he worked in an office and not as a dockworker that he escaped Tunny's scrutiny. Scheindl continued to supply Koeing with details of Allied purchase orders, including sailing orders for ships carrying those cargos.

*   *   *

Ben Stent had been inactive since the Imperoyl fiasco in February, which had depleted him almost entirely of his remaining stock of cigar bombs. There had been no further contact with Paul Koeing since his arrest the previous December. Because of the security crackdown in New York, he had been unable to make contact with anyone who could help him acquire a new shipment of cigar bombs.

A week earlier, Ben had been sitting alone in the Pig's Revenge. It was early on a Friday evening and he was nursing his third Keith's Ale after his early supper. A hot turkey sandwich, one of the most popular dishes on the Pig's menu. *Oh, what I would give for some real German sausages, sauerkraut and boiled potatoes*, he thought with self-pity.

As he sat there trying to drink himself out of a depression that had been plaguing him for several days, he noticed a man sitting by himself at a corner table. Was it Ben's imagination, or was the guy sizing him up? As he was thinking that, the man got up and hesitantly approached Ben's table.

The man looked to be in his late forties, with tired watery eyes, short grey hair and a drinker's nose. He tipped his glass to Ben by way of greeting. "Do you mind if I join you?" he whispered with his beery breath.

Besides being naturally suspicious of strangers, Ben wasn't in the mood. "I've noticed your glances. You seemed to be watching me. What d'you want?"

"Well, if your name is Ruben Stendt, I would welcome the opportunity to talk to you."

"Are you a cop? No, you don't look like a cop."

"I'm not a cop. I don't work for anyone who might have an interest in you. I'm just a stranger visiting your city for a few days."

"From?"

"New York. My name is Pieter, spelled P-i-e-t-e-r."

"OK. Have a seat. Who sent you to see me?"

"Friends." He whispered close to Ben. "Does the name Paul Koeing mean anything to you?"

"I heard he got arrested last year. I wasn't friends with him."

"Let's just say you had an association with him. Don't worry, I'm not an investigator or anything like that. I just want to establish my bona fides. I've a proposal for you."

Ben finished his pint and ordered his fourth. "And one for my friend."

"Just a half, please."

"Tell me what you know about me."

"First, I was born in New York. Both of my parents were from the old country. I have always felt more German than American. I guess my anti-American feelings are what aroused the interest of Paul. He recruited me, but kept me in the background. I think he was worried about my drinking. After von Rintelen's deportation and Paul's arrest, I laid low for a long time."

"What's that got to do with me?"

"I heard about your operation here from a friend who was also a good friend of Paul's. This friend was also part of a secret network that Paul did not know about. When Paul's network disappeared, this friend became more active in the other secret network. Recently, this network came into possession of some very important information and since it directly relates to Halifax, I was recruited by my friend to pay you a visit here."

"I'm still in the dark. Are you offering me a role in some operation?"

"Let's just say a partnership. Most of the planning has been done, but the final piece of the operation has to be carried out in Halifax. That's where you come in. I'm here to invite you to a meeting in New York."

*   *   *

That had been a week ago, and now here he was on the second of November, sitting at the Café Bismarck on 86th Street at nine o' clock on a Friday night. Wearing a black toque and a red scarf, as instructed. The Café Bismarck was located in the heart of Yorkville, a very German ghetto where German sausage shops lined the streets and German newspapers were sold at newsstands. The locals often celebrated German victories on the European front with Rhine wine. The pub also served large steins of cheap German beer.

It seemed to Ben as if he were back in Germany. Most of the conversation around him was in German.

"Well, you do look German. You don't look like a Canuck," said the barrel-bellied man as he drew a chair up to Ben's table.

"I thought the toque would identify me as a Canadian," Ben said with an air of frustration. He had been sitting here for over an hour wondering if anyone was going to meet him. All he had was Pieter's word. No telephone number. No contact address.

"Pleased to make your acquaintance. My name is Frederick Hinsch. Captain Hinsch. You can call me Captain. That's what most people call me." All this was said with a gruff manner. It was as if he was used to being the boss. The one in control.

"And my name is Ruben Stendt. Everyone calls be Ben." Ben could hear an accordion player start up in an adjoining room. Add that to the smoky atmosphere and strong smell of beer and sauerkraut, and he could well be back in Germany.

"As you know Ben, things have been bit unsettled here since Black Tom. And what with our bomb expert fleeing to Mexico, production has been severely limited."

"I know, because I never did receive the shipment Paul promised to send me last year."

"It's just as well. So many of Walter Scheele's undetonated cigars have been discovered in the past year that the police and even many dockhands knew what they were when they saw them. The German government didn't sit idly by during this time, but improved on the design.

"Listen, Ben, this is not the place to discuss our plan and how it involves you. We need to meet in a more secure place. My real goal in meeting you tonight was to check you out. There are so many undercover police out there, I had to be sure. I am confident you are who you say you are. One last question, who is your assistant in Canada?"

"Danny Sullivan. Am I cleared now?"

"I trust you, Ben. Until I hear otherwise. I've arranged a room for you in a nice brownstone not far from here. Martha Held is the matron there, and you might be interested in her services. I will meet you there sometime tomorrow afternoon."

"I'll be waiting for you, Captain." Ben wasn't sure what to think about this captain. He exuded an air of intimidation, but Ben had no intention of feeling intimidated. *As long as I'm not treated like the hired help, I welcome all the support you can give me. But I am running the show in Halifax.*

55

3 November 1917. New York.

IT WAS PAST ONE O'CLOCK WHEN BEN FINISHED HIS lunch. *That was the finest Reuben sandwich I have ever tasted*, he declared to himself. Real sauerkraut, real Russian dressing. *And I am proud for having been named after this famous sandwich, if indeed I was.*

His meeting with the captain was set for two o'clock back at the 'boarding' house, about a twenty-minute walk from this bustling little restaurant that had been recommended by the madame. A good brisk walk in the crisp, salty air was just what he needed to clear out the cobwebs still lingering after his late-night encounter with the alcohol spirits.

Captain Hinsch was waiting for him. He was accompanied by a well-groomed man in his early fifties whose posture bore witness to a military background. His round wire spectacles sat below two bushy eyebrows. Thinning hair started halfway back from his shining, bald forehead.

Ben was ushered into a small, windowless basement room at the rear of the house. "Ben, this is Hans Marguerre. He is a German citizen who has been sent here to continue the work of Walter Scheele, who, as you know, fled the country last year. He has something to show you. And then we'll explain how our plan involves you."

"You're accustomed to Walter's cigars, because I know you have successfully used them," said Marguerre. "These new bombs are an improvement on Walter's design and are now manufactured in Germany. They are brought over by submarine." From a satchel he had brought with him, Marguerre pulled out a small box the size of a cigar box. He lifted the lid to reveal what appeared to be an assortment of red, green and blue coloured pencils. "My crayons," he exclaimed proudly. "No one has ever seen these pencils before."

The outer shell was made of thick coloured glass. Inside were the same chemical-filled compartments used in Scheele's cigars. "The different colours represent the different lengths of time from activation to ignition. This blue one, for instance, has a six-day fuse. We are told that these new bombs will be even more effective than Walter's bombs."

"How safe are they to handle?" Ben asked.

"Good question, my friend. Under normal handling conditions, they are as safe as the bombs you are used to. Unless this box were to be subjected to a violent blow that damaged the glass tubes, there is little danger of an explosion. See that rubber stopper covering the copper plug in the middle of the tube? When you pull that little lever on the upper side of the tube, it lifts a thin wire inside the tube. That wire is connected to the rubber gasket, and when that is released, sulfuric acid begins eating at the copper plug. The bomb is now armed."

"You see Ben," Hinsch interjected, "pretty much what you're used to. Now, let's get down to business."

Letting out a long sigh of expectation, Ben replied, "That's why I am here."

"Before we begin, I to need impress upon you that this mission I'm about to describe has been given high priority directly by Berlin. Not only is the cargo a significant target, but the German government wishes to demonstrate that German saboteurs active not only on the American waterfront, but also on the Canadian waterfront. No place is safe from their reach."

"As you know," said Ben, "we had a few successes last year. But we haven't been able to stock up on bombs since the beginning of this year. It would be great to signal our return with a spectacular statement."

"Let me continue." Hinsch said. As you know, we have a source in the National City Bank who provides us with information on ships and their cargos. That agent is still in place and he has found a target for our continuing campaign."

"And I gather that you have found out that the target ship is heading to Halifax in the near future?"

"That is so, Ben. But this ship is not just carrying war supplies for the Allies, this ship will be loaded to the gills with all kinds of explosives. A floating bomb. The ship is called the *Mont Blanc*, and has been commissioned by the French government to deliver its deadly cargo to France. It will be arriving in New York sometime during the next week. Loading the explosives will take two or three weeks. We expect the ship to leave New York by the end of November. It'll head to Halifax, where it will join a British convoy."

"Will the ship be taking on additional supplies in Halifax? I mean, how are any dock workers going to get aboard the ship?"

Hinsch replied with a loud sigh, "security is so tight here in New York we don't have any chance of planting any bombs on that ship. And regards your question about dockworkers in Halifax, I can tell you they won't have an opportunity either."

Ben knitted his eyebrows and stared at Hinch, "is the ship taking on any supplies at all in Halifax at all?"

"No. It'll be fully laden when it leaves New York. When it

reaches Halifax, it will be anchored in Bedford Basin, where it will be assigned a place in the convoy leaving later that week. You will have maybe two or three days from that point to plant your bombs."

"Captain, I have two obvious questions. How do we get the bombs from here to Halifax? And, more important, how do we get them aboard the ship while it's in the Basin?"

"To answer your first question, you're going to take a small supply of pencil bombs back with you tomorrow. Ten of those bombs should be enough. We've prepared a shipment of five boxes of cigars, which you will easily be able to carry on board the train back to Canada. We have also prepared some paperwork, including a business card, identifying you as the representative of a cigar company headquartered in New York. You're taking this small supply of cigars back to Halifax to see if you can establish a market in Canada for these fine Cuban cigars."

"I assume that if anyone wants to open one of those boxes, all he would see are cigars?"

Two of the boxes have false bottoms. So, to answer your question, yes all they will see are cigars. Don't forget, customs officials do inspections on board, not when you disembark in Halifax. They don't have a lot of room to do anything but a cursory inspection. And they always seem to be in a hurry."

"Well, I hope you're right."

"Your target is the *Mont Blanc*. It's expected to arrive in Halifax on Wednesday, the fifth of December. She will take on a pilot who will steer the ship along the harbour and to her berth in Bedford Basin. The convoy will have been organized by then and will be ready to leave on Friday.

That same pilot who steered the ship in will also steer the ship out. The pilot will have an assistant with him on Friday. Someone who is being trained by the pilot. That assistant will plant the bombs. He won't even have to go below decks, as the main deck will be crammed with barrels of benzene, with plenty of spaces to quickly hide a small bag of cigars."

"And why is this pilot going to take along an assistant?"

"Because he won't want anything to happen to his wife or children. We have two men who will be travelling to Halifax on the weekend. Two Irishmen supplied by our IRA brethren. With your help they'll ensure the pilot's cooperation. These men will need a place to stay and a guide to familiarize them with the lay of the land. You're going to help them get organized. Make sure they know all about the pilot, where he lives and how he gets ready for his assignments."

"Are you saying that I will be invisible to any investigations into this ship, the *Mont Blanc*, exploding at sea?"

"Correct. Your role will keep you behind the scenes. Neither the pilot nor his family will know about you. Once the job is finished these guys will restrain the pilot in a secure location. They will put the fear of God into him with future threats to his family. By the time the *Mont Blanc* clears Halifax Harbour, our men will be settling into their train seats for their return journey back to New York. Your job will be to release the pilot later in the afternoon. Make sure he won't be able to identify you."

Ben had a good feeling that this plan was going to work. *I'll need Danny's help with this, but in a limited role. I just don't trust him to keep his mouth shut. He can babysit the two Irishmen.*

56

2 December 1917. Halifax.

ON FRIDAY, INSPECTOR TUNNY'S BOMB SQUAD ARRESTED Frederick Scheindl on charges of espionage and abetting German sabotage activity. Scheindl had long been an agent of Paul Koeing, and continued surveillance of Koeing had led them to Scheindl.

Since Koeing's arrest a year ago, in December 1916, Scheindl had lain low and had not been in contact with any of Koeing's agents. That had changed in November when Captain Hinsch had rekindled the partnership. Tunny's investigators had gleaned rumours of Scheindl's activities, but had not been able to find any evidence about the dormant agent's spying activities. They had kept a careful watch on him and were delighted when he was observed having a walk in Central Park with Captain Hinsch.

The investigators were provided with search warrants and were able to uncover a list of all Allied telegrams transmitted to the bank for the purchase of war materials since the beginning of the year. All of these telegrams had passed through Scheindl's hands. Included on this list was the cargo and destination of the *Mont Blanc*.

It was early on Sunday afternoon when Tunny himself called the Halifax chief of police at home. He had called the station-house, and had to put the fear of God into the duty sergeant before he would release Captain Gallagher's phone number.

"Hello, Captain Gallagher, I apologize for calling you at home, especially on a Sunday. I would've waited until tomorrow when you were at work, but I deemed it too urgent to wait." Tunny had spewed out all of this greeting before Gallagher has said no more then "Hello."

"My name is Thomas Tunny, and I'm an inspector with the New York Police Department."

"Good morning, inspector. I was just sitting here with my wife, enjoying a bit of warmth in front of the grate. It's cold out here today. What's so urgent that it can't wait?"

"First of all, captain, I would like to extend my apologies to your duty sergeant. I had to bully him into providing your phone number. But this call really is urgent."

"That's all right, Inspector. I'm a policeman every day of the week. Does this have anything to do with the war?"

"It has everything to do with the war. I'm in charge of the New York bomb squad. We're one of the agencies set up after Black Tom was blown up."

"I'm well aware of Black Tom," Gallagher replied.

"After the explosion we reorganized the bomb squad to focus on a specific goal. We intend to crush an active ring of German agents and saboteurs operating in New York and New Jersey. Let me explain." Tunny went on to describe how they found out about the *Mont Blanc* and her cargo. "We have evidence that the *Mont Blanc* was to be a target in New York, but that changed due to very tight security. We now believe that these saboteurs are focusing their resources on attacking this ship while it is in Halifax."

"Have you alerted the captain of the *Mont Blanc* about that threat? He surely would need to take extra precautions."

"Too late for that, Captain, the *Mont Blanc* set sail yesterday morning. This ship appears to be a strategic target for these bastards who want to demonstrate their reach against American interests."

Gallagher wondered why the inspector had called the chief of police instead of the admiralty. "As soon as we finish this call I will be in touch with the admiralty. It will be their responsibility to secure protection for the *Mont Blanc*."

"Which brings me to the reason I called you first and not the admiralty. Being an American of Irish descent, I have always stayed in close contact with the Irish community here in New York. Long before this war started, I had developed a reliable network of agents and snitches within the community. You could visit whole sections of this city and swear you were in Ireland."

Tunny continued, "With all the local support for the Irish nationalists waging their terrorist activities in the old country, we often found ourselves keeping track of IRA supporters here in America. A lot them express more sympathy towards Germany than Britain."

"I know, Inspector, because we see the same support here among our own Irish population."

"That doesn't surprise me, Captain. So, you will understand when I tell you that we have acquired reliable knowledge of two Irish thugs who are rumoured to have left for Canada to do a job."

"You mean, they are going to attack the *Mont Blanc* here in Halifax?"

"We suspect that. So, I am making a formal request to you to be on the lookout for them. Their names are McEwan and Doherty, and there's no mistaking their Irish accents. Just discretely keep an eye on them. I don't want them to get any suspicions they are being watched."

"Rest assured, Inspector Tunny, I'll have men at the railway station first thing in the morning. Assuming those two have not already arrived, we'll post lookouts for the whole week if necessary. We'll spot them."

"Thank you, Captain, I really appreciate your help. And I hope the rest of your day goes without interruption."

57

3 December 1917. Halifax.

IT WAS DARK WHEN DANNY ARRIVED AT BEN'S SALTBOX house. He was accompanied by the two Irishmen from New York. He had had no problem recognizing the two thugs. Although he didn't have a photograph, he easily picked them out of the crowd of disembarking passengers on the 5:20 PM train. They *looked* Irish. And they looked suspicious, with furtive glances on the lookout for trouble.

Danny had approached the pair, and emphasizing his Irish brogue said, "If you're new to Halifax and looking for a nice clean hotel, I am here to offer you a ride to one of the city's finest establishments." That's all it took.

Ben was quick to usher them inside. He didn't want any nosy neighbors witnessing their arrival. "This is Colin Doherty, and this here is Sean McEwan" Danny introduced the two men.

"Come in, Come in." Ben led them into the kitchen. "I've been expecting you. I've even stocked some Guinness for your arrival. And you can stay here for the night. We can sort out other accommodation later."

Ben's kitchen was the largest room in the house. Also the warmest. The four men had plenty of room sitting around the kitchen table.

McEwen was the talker. He was sullen and made no bones about not wanting to be here. "We thought the boat would be here by now. The Captain said it wouldn't be more than three or four days."

"The convoy is expected to leave on Friday," said Ben with a shrug. Our work will be done by then and you will be on the 1:00 PM train heading back to the U.S. "So, four more days. You OK with that?"

"I suppose. Maybe we could grab a piece of tail during that time."

"Let me tell you straight up, fellows. You do not want to draw any attention to yourselves." Ben uttered these words with menace in his voice. His cold gray eyes did not invite any argument. "I'll try and accommodate you as best I can."

"It's your show, mate. We are here to lend a helping hand. We've been briefed by the Captain, but I also want to hear the plan from you directly, so we understand each other's roles."

"What exactly did Captain Hinsch tell you?"

"He said one of us will hold the pilot's family hostage the night before the convoy sails. The other one, probably me, will accompany the pilot aboard the *Mont Blanc* as his assistant. My job is to plant the cigars somewhere on deck amongst all the barrels there, so they will not be detected."

Ben replied, "The pilot will be taking you on board the *Mont Blanc* very early on Friday morning, and will explain to the captain that you are a journeyman pilot and that this is part of your education experience."

McEwan nodded his understanding. "While I'm doing that, my friend here will hold the pilot's family hostage beginning on Thursday night. When the mission is complete, we will tie up the pilot and his family with a promise that they will be released sometime the next day. By then Colin and I will be on board the afternoon train heading back to New York."

"Yeah, that's pretty much it."

"I also understand," McEwan continued, "that your red-headed friend here will look after our needs for the next couple of days." We'll need a driver and someone who knows his way around. Oh, and one more thing. The captain said you would provide us with a revolver. It's only for show. We don't intend to shoot anyone."

"Correct. Danny will be your escort. He brought you here today, and he'll deliver you to the train station on Friday and make sure your train tickets are in order. He can also arrange for a visit to a brothel. Maybe Wednesday night for that. Anything else you need, like meals or liquor, Danny will also arrange. He will also supply you with a revolver."

"One other thing," Ben continued. "I want to make this clear. When you are on board the *Mont Blanc* with the pilot, I don't want him or anyone else to see you planting the bombs. No one, especially the pilot, must know what you are doing. If someone raises an alarm after the ship sets sail, this mission will be a total failure."

"Understood."

"The ship we are targeting arrives in Halifax on Wednesday and will be anchored in Bedford Basin until Friday. She will be leaving early Friday morning as part of a convoy heading to France and England. The harbour pilot that brings her into Halifax harbour will be the same pilot who takes her back out of the harbour, where she will form up with convoy."

"Are you going to help us with the hostage taking?"

" On Thursday night Danny will drop both of you off at the pilot's house. He has a wife and three young children. You two will force yourself into the house, and brandishing the revolver, you will keep everyone secure for the night. No violence!"

"Will youse guys be with us?"

"No. It is imperative that neither Danny nor myself be seen by the family. We don't want them identifying us after the fact. Another thing—don't mention anything to the pilot. He doesn't know anything about his role on Friday morning. Around four in the morning one of you will escort him to an address I will provide. There, you put the fear of God into him. Make sure he knows precisely what will happen to his family if he doesn't fully cooperate. And give him his instructions."

58

4 December 1917. Halifax.

IT WAS STILL DARK WHEN HARRY ARRIVED AT THE STA-
tion. Captain Gallagher was already sitting at their meeting table.
Sandy had not yet made it in. "Good morning, Mike. Guess we
have our work cut out for us."

Just then, Sandy stuck his head in the door. In a breathless
whisper he said, "Sorry I'm late. The wife has come down with a
cold or the flu. Whatever it is, she's sick as a dog. I told her to stay
in bed for a day or two."

Harry stood up. "Come in and have a seat. I just made a pot of
tea, and I've got some apple muffins Liz made yesterday."

Mike summarized the events of the past twenty-four hours.
He started with the phone call from Inspector Tunny on Sunday.
"It sure was timely. If he hadn't called when he did, we would've
missed those two Irishmen from New York. It certainly allowed us
time to get you in place at the train station, Sandy. Any comments
about that?"

Sandy paused, as he was about to take a bite of his muffin.
"It's lucky Harry didn't go on the stakeout. He would have been
recognized by our own Irish suspect. Danny Sullivan has never
laid eyes on me, but he would've noticed Harry."

Sandy put his muffin back down but took a long drink of his
tea. He continued. "When we got together yesterday morning to

organize our strategy, we agreed to send someone to the Nova Scotian Hotel to keep an eye out for suspicious characters arriving on the afternoon train from New York. The restaurant in the hotel is a perfect vantage point overlooking the arrivals platform. I was able to get an out-of-the-way table, and I brought a newspaper as added concealment if I needed it."

"Weren't the hotel staff suspicious of you loitering around?" asked Harry.

"Of course not. Don't forget, a lot of people wait in the restaurant when they are there to meet passengers. We had a bit of luck on our side, gentlemen. Who shows up but Danny Sullivan. He was easy to spot with that receding mop of curly red hair. It takes him a few minutes, but he eventually identifies the two Irishmen he is there to collect."

"Mike, with all your insistence on evidence—not that I disagree with you, but Holy Cow—you got to admit that circumstantial evidence does play a mighty role in the quest for justice." Harry uttered these words as his justification for the *what-if* speculations that he constantly used as a road map to the truth. Speculations he was always bouncing off of Sandy, and even his wife.

"You and I are in complete agreement, Harry. A good imagination can lead us to the truth. Take all those little bits of the puzzle and lay them on a board. Eventually some of them are going to fit together and a picture will be revealed."

Sandy said, "Danny seems to be a key piece of the puzzle. He works with this Stendt fellow in the dockyards. Packy has seen them drinking together at the Pig, not to mention Packy and Rita seeing them on Citadel Hill paying close attention to that ship entering the harbour—the ship that sank a week later at sea in the middle of a convoy. Plus, we've heard from several sources about Danny's rants about the Americans supplying Germany's enemies with war materials when they were supposedly a neutral country in the war."

"Absolutely correct," Harry replied. "And now we have Danny collecting two Irishmen from New York that Inspector Tunny told us to watch out for."

"Not to mention Tunny's warning about a possible attempt to sabotage the *Mont Blanc* in Halifax," added Mike. "By the way, that ship is due here sometime tomorrow, and should be anchored in the basin by tomorrow evening. What are your thoughts, Harry? Do you think they might try something while she sits at anchor?"

"Maybe. I mean, the two boys from New York are here, but I don't see how they could get near the ship if she stays anchored in the basin. Especially if we alert the captain to keep an extra vigilant lookout while he's at anchor."

"Of course, Harry's right," Mike emphasized. "But, what if this Stendt guy figured out a way to fool the captain into believing something that would allow Stendt to be invited aboard?"

Sandy was absorbing this line of thought. "Good idea. Maybe a medical inspection? Suppose there was a smallpox rumour going around, and this sudden medical inspection was just an alert to determine if the crew was at risk and if they needed to take extra precautions to safeguard the crew."

Mike said, "I like the way you guys think. Keep at it. Keep thinking more *what ifs*. Anything, no matter how absurd or foolish it may sound. In the meantime, Harry, get a couple of men to keep an eye on that house and those Irishmen. See where they go. And especially that Sullivan guy. He's probably the errand guy. We've got to stay focused on the belief that there will be an attempt to destroy the *Mont Blanc*.

59

4 December 1917.
Off the coast of Nova Scotia.

THE *MONT BLANC* HAD LEFT NEW YORK THREE DAYS AGO, on Saturday, at precisely at 11:11 AM. The weather was cold and battleship gray, just like the colour of the ship. And just like the mood of the crew. Today, the mood had somewhat improved, mainly because of the weather. The sun was shining, the sky was as beautiful as the vault of heaven should be, and the sea a carpet of gentle waves. For two days they'd been battered by a northwest gale, which had slowed their passage to Halifax.

Aimé and Jean were standing on the ship's prow. Ordinarily it would have been too windy to carry on a conversation here, but today there was no wind. They were standing together at the rail wedged in by the drums of benzene. The life boats and drums took up almost all the free space on deck.

"Finally, a nice day, my friend," Jean smiled and lifted up his face to the bright sun. The breeze was so subtle it felt like a soft caress from his wife.

Aimé looked him intently in the eye. "Aye, it's been a rough two days. There's not much room on deck, but I want you to make sure everyone who wants to has a chance to come out here."

"Now that you mention it, I think I will organize a series of inspection crews. Maybe five at a time. Over eight hours that will accommodate everyone. They can thoroughly inspect all the drums and make sure nothing has come the least bit loose from the deck rails. That really hasn't been possible since we left New York. And check the life boat covers as well. I can see two from right here that need tightening up."

"How do the men seem to you, Jean? I mean their spirits."

"I think they are stoic, Aimé. Like the British are fond of saying, keeping a stiff upper lip. They are all yearning to be home for Christmas, but at the same time they worry about being sighted by German U-boats. They live with that menace on their minds every waking moment. Even so, the only thing they grumble about is not being able to smoke."

"I am sure no one misses their pipe more than you, Jean. When we reach Halifax, I hope we can arrange shore leave for at least some of the men. I hope. And, the terrible weather we have had for the last two days has made it harder for prowling U-boats to find us."

"Speaking of prowling U-boats, they are looking for a single ship, right? Do you think, Aimé, that we will be harder to find if we can make it into the convoy?"

"I have thought about that a lot. In a convoy there would be quite a few ships for the U-boat captain to choose from. Unless we had a target painted on our hull, say a red flag, why would they choose us over any other ship in the convoy? And don't forget, we would have the protection afforded to the convoy from those heavily armed battleships."

Aimé stroked his thick black mustache and carefully trimmed goatee. This bushy thicket of facial hair gave him presence and projected an air of authority. His erect stance and dark eyes betrayed a serious man. A smaller version of Joseph Conrad. He thought again about the conversation he had had with Flowers and

Commander Coates, the convoy officer in the British Admiralty Office in New York. The three men had discussed details of the arrangements for the *Mont Blanc*'s inclusion in the convoy leaving Halifax.

There had been some heated discussion about rejecting the *Mont Blanc*'s inclusion in the convoy because she was too slow. When Commander Coates had asked Aimé if he could make 200 miles a day to maintain pace with the convoy, he had nodded slowly and said, "I think we could do that in good weather." To which Coates had muttered, "I'll have to see about that."

In the end, Coates had decided to leave the decision to the navel authorities in Halifax. If the *Mont Blanc* was not to be included, Captain Le Médec would receive sealed orders from the admiralty in Halifax providing the secret route he should follow across the Atlantic.

These thoughts were interrupted by the first officer.

"Sir. We have just sighted land."

"Ah! Jean, that's the coast of Nova Scotia. If we don't lose any more time, we should be docked in Halifax by tomorrow evening."

"That is good news, Aimé. I will announce it to the crew."

The captain dreaded the Admiralty's decision about being included in the convoy, but kept those fears to himself. If our orders are to sail solo back to France, we will have no choice but to comply.

60

5 December 1917. Halifax.

FRANCIS MACKEY LIVED IN HERRING COVE. FROM HIS BACK veranda he could see all the way up past George's Island, where he worked as a harbour pilot out of Pier 6. Hale and hearty at 45, Mackey had already spent 24 years on the water, most of them as one the harbour's more experienced pilots. It was cool on his veranda, and he knew he would have to dress warmly for the day ahead. He finished his cigarette and flicked the butt toward the water, but a curl of wind caught it and dumped it on the rocks to the right of his house. He took a last gulp of his tea and went inside for the rest of his morning ritual with his wife and kids.

Mackey didn't have many vices, unless you called a love for cigars a vice. He was of medium height but as fit as a fiddle. A sea-faring man, he had a weathered face that could host a serious expression when the occasion called for a by-the-book response to a problem. That was often the case in his job piloting all kinds of ships in and out of Halifax's busy war-time harbour. Too much traffic, and regulations being dangerously relaxed to accommodate the 'war effort.' The highlight of today's agenda was an ammunition ship arriving from New York to be berthed in Bedford Basin for the upcoming convoy to England.

"Morning, George," he greeted his neighbour who picked him

up every morning at seven for their drive to Pier 6, where they both started their day's work.

"Mornin'," replied George. "Think it'll be choppy today?"

Mackey climbed into the passenger seat and plopped his lunch pail on the floor. "Not too bad, I think. Just hope it's not so busy as it seems to have become every day."

"Sure, it's busy and I appreciate that. What with the war and all. But everything's rushed. Got to be done by yesterday. It's dangerous the way a lot of those boats exceed the harbour speed limit. I see small collisions almost every day. Or near-collisions."

"I agree. If only people would follow the rules of the road."

"I can tell you that there's going to be a serious collision someday. And I don't mean a small boat hitting the ferry. I just hope it doesn't happen on my watch."

61

5 December 1917. Halifax.

NOON FOUND HARRY SITTING IN ONE OF THE POLICE cruisers parked on top of Citadel Hill. The sky was such a pale colour of blue it was almost white. And the wind was cold. That's why he had the heater jacked up. His eyes tracked the route of the harbour north past Georges Island, up past the sugar refinery to the Narrows, where it curved left and emptied into Bedford Basin. The same route the *Mont Blanc*, like every ship before her, travelled to the shelter of the Basin.

The *Mont Blanc* was due sometime today. No one could tell him exactly what time, but he thought he would go up the hill and take a look. Maybe he'd be lucky and see her enter the harbour over by Chebucto Head. If she was going to be a target, he wanted to have good look at her. See what this ammunitions ship looked like. He had a general description of her, but he was told the red flag she was flying would be the dead giveaway that she was carrying explosives.

Harry scratched his nose and thought back to breakfast earlier that morning. Bacon, eggs, toast and tea. Certainly not his usual breakfast. Far from it. But today was a special day for Milly, and the breakfast was in her honour.

Her class was meeting down at St. Thomas Aquinas Church. Under the direction of her Uncle Pete, the parish priest, she was going to help organize a Christmas drive for the poor and needy. For the next two days the students were going to go door knocking down in the South End asking for donations. Liz thought Milly should have a hearty breakfast so she would have lots of energy for the day ahead.

Harry was the lucky beneficiary of Milly's good fortune. While Liz fussed over her daughter Harry kept pestering her with questions. He couldn't stop thinking about the *Mont Blanc* and how she could be attacked in Bedford Basin.

"This ship's not going to be docked anywhere along the waterfront. They're not taking on any additional cargo."

"Well Harry, my dear, doesn't that solve your problems?" Liz said this matter-of-factly.

"Some, but I can't stop thinking of other ways the ship could be attacked."

"You mean by another boat? A small one? Or are you thinking about a swimmer? Someone who could approach the ship unnoticed, climb up on the deck and plant a bomb and return to the water?"

"No, Liz. Not another boat. And not a swimmer. Anyway, I don't think these saboteurs want to cause an explosion here in Halifax. I think they want to plant explosives that will detonate several days after the ship leaves Halifax. Like the other three ships that left here and exploded at sea."

"You mean somebody's going to sneak aboard?"

"I suppose they could, but we're going to insist on very tight security aboard that ship while she is in Halifax. So, possible, but very unlikely."

"All right, Harry, then somebody has to find a way of being invited aboard."

Harry had been thinking along those lines all morning, but

grew more frustrated the more he thought about it. Now it was noon and he hadn't come up with a single idea. He kept thinking about Liz's idea about someone being invited.

All of a sudden Harry slapped the side of his head. *Eureka!* What if someone demanded that the captain of the *Mont Blanc* allow a navel authority, for example, to be invited aboard? Maybe for an inspection or something? Or what if someone were held hostage to force a person with a legitimate reason to board the ship to take an accomplice aboard with him? Like bank robbers do during a bank robbery. *Naw*, he thought, *then the saboteur would be known to the authorities and his plot would fail.* So, food for thought. How could a saboteur get aboard and escape detection after planting his bombs?

62

5 December 1917. Halifax.

DAYLIGHT WAS STARTING TO WANE AS FRANCIS MACKEY climbed aboard the *Mont Blanc* from an outgoing pilot boat. He scrambled up the ladder and pulled himself on deck, where he was greeted by Captain Aimé Le Médec in halting English. Eleven years ago, Le Médec had studied English for his captain's exam, but he rarely spoke it now, and to tell the truth he was very self-conscious about speaking it. "Welcome aboard the *Mont Blanc*. I apologize for not speaking your language so well. I will do my best."

The captain led Mackey to the bridge and introduced him to his wheelsman, Alphonse Serré, and Second Lieutenant Joseph Levesque.

Serré was at the wheel and Levesque sat at his right, in control of the whistle cord that was used to transmit orders to the engine room.

Mackey thought it unlikely that the ship would be allowed to enter the harbour this late in the day, but he kept this to himself until he received official instructions from the Examination Boat. "Captain, please ask your helmsman to proceed past the lighthouse to that ship anchored there. We'll be boarded by an examining officer."

"Of course, Mr. Mackey." He then barked out an order in French.

Examining Officer Terrance Freeman crossed to the *Mont Blanc* on a lighter and made his way to the bridge, where he was introduced to everyone. "Welcome to Halifax. I've come to examine your manifest papers, please." He glanced at the bow, where five hundred canvas straps bound iron barrels to the deck.

As Le Médec handed over the papers he remarked, "We are all explosives."

Freeman had never seen a cargo like the one on the *Mont Blanc*. He knew the war had made increased demands on the old port city. A lot more traffic and an easement of some harbour regulations, maybe too much so. Like the red flag that was supposed to be flown by any ammunition ship entering the harbour. Up until now, there were relatively few ammunition ships that had entered the harbour, but the Mont Blanc was the first one with permission to sail all the way to Bedford Basin.

As Freeman continued down the list of explosives on the manifest he declared, "You have a very dangerous cargo, Captain. I'd hate to imagine what would happen if there were an accident. I know we all have to take increased risks for the war effort, but this? And you are not even flying a red flag!"

"Sir," Le Médec answered, "we've just spent four days alone on the Atlantic Ocean on our voyage from New York. We had no protection from any prowling German submarines. We would've been doomed if we'd been sighted. A red flag would have announced our cargo. It would've made us a target. Our office has given us permission to dispense with the red flag even here in Halifax, where we are still a target." He might have had difficulty with his English, but he did get his point across. He did not want to fly that flag.

"Well, if the military authorities—and I mean the British Admiralty who are in charge—are giving you permission, my only advice to you is to be very careful. However, I'm afraid you won't be able to go into the Basin today. It's too late in the day. I know there's still a lot of light in the sky, but they have closed the submarine gates already."

Halifax had two submarine nets. Both stretched on either side of George's Island to the opposite shore. They were opened and closed at random times to allow scheduled ships into the harbour and to prevent German submarines from sneaking into the outer harbour. The mesh gates were anchored to the harbour floor by three-ton concrete weights. When they slammed shut at night, they sent a shiver along the buoys that marked their presence.

Freeman gave them their instructions. "Unless you hear differently from me in the morning, you can proceed up the harbour as soon as you are able. The gates will be opened around 7:30. Good luck."

After Freeman had left the ship, Mackey joined the captain and two senior officers—Glotin, who spoke fluent English, and Leveque. Mackey told Le Médec that he would prefer to spend the night aboard rather than return home. He told them this often happened and his wife was quite used to it. That way they could get an early start.

Glotin began to recount their experience in New York. He told Mackey about all the protective measures that took place in the loading of the cargo. After their evening meal was finished and coffee was served, Mackey offered cigars to the three men. Le Médec abruptly stood up and with wide, fearful eyes rasped, "You cannot smoke on this ship! All tobacco and matches are banned."

With Glotin's help, the captain went on to recount his conversation with officers in the British Admiralty offices in New York.

"We were asked about the speed of our ship and would we be able to keep up with the convoy. The *Mont Blanc* is a very old vessel, Mr. Mackey, and it's slow. We have only one screw, and even travelling in ballast we can barely mange thirteen knots. In normal times the owners would never use it to carry such a dangerous cargo."

"Aye. But these are not normal times are they, Captain?"

"It seems the French government is in such need of war supplies they'll use any ship at their disposal to transport what is needed. Including the *Mont Blanc*. Add the weight of our cargo, and the ship is even slower than usual. The Admiralty has instructed the convoy officer to give me a sealed envelope that can only be opened in the event that we lose sight of the convoy. There will be instructions outlining the route home if we should have to proceed on our own."

"My God, Captain, how do you ever sleep at night?"

63

6 December 1917. Halifax.

THE SS *IMO* WAS A NORWEGIAN CARGO STEAMSHIP THAT had been contracted by the Commission for Belgium Relief to pick up supplies in New York. It had a crew of 37 men commanded by Captain Haakon From. Nearly everyone was Norwegian.

The *Imo* was a long and narrow ship. Because it had no cargo her rudder and propeller were nearly out of the water, making her hard to steer. This made it difficult to maneuver, especially in tight quarters like the Narrows of Halifax Harbour.

The ship had been in Bedford Basin for three days and had been given clearance to depart Halifax the day before, on Wednesday. Her departure had been delayed because her coal supply had been delivered too late in the day, after the submarine nets had been closed for the night. Now it was Thursday and Captain From was furious because of the delay.

*   *   *

On 6 December the Catholic Church celebrated the feast day of St. Nicholas. It was Thursday, a school day, and Liz's brother, Father Pete, was celebrating the feast day with a special mass at 8:00 AM to honour St. Nicholas as the patron saint of Christmas. Since Milly was going back to St. Thomas Aquinas for her second day of gathering donations, Liz thought she'd go with her to help out. They could attend the mass beforehand.

Not wanting to miss out on this opportunity to share Christmas memories with his family, Harry said he'd go as well. "Besides, I won't be going into the station until ten o'clock anyway. Sandy's wife is still confined to bed with a bit of a fever, and I told Sandy to look after her until ten. I told him I'd pick him up then, and we could drive into the office together."

*   *   *

Pier 8 was a beehive of activity. Three ships were scheduled to be loaded with cargos bound for France. And they had to be fully loaded without fail, as the convoy was scheduled to leave Halifax early Friday morning. Ben Stendt and Danny Sullivan were committed to a full day's work. They had started work at the stroke of seven, and by eight-thirty they were enjoying a lull in the work due to a malfunctioning crane on the ship they were loading.

Leaning against a pillar, Ben and Danny were having a quiet smoke near the edge of the wooden pier. "I guess we'll soon be seeing that ammunition ship going past," Danny offered.

Ben took a long pull on his pipe and used it as a pointer to show where the *Mont Blanc* was already heading past George's Island. "Should be going past here before nine. We'll get a good look at her then."

"Well, we're ready. Those two Irish guys said they'd go down to the waterfront to watch it come in. They're anxious for this job to be over with and be on their way back to New York."

"Long as they do their job, Danny, and you drive them back to the station, they should be gone from Halifax before the noon gun goes off on Friday."

*   *   *

Francis Mackey was ready for the day's work. Before heading up to the bridge he'd found just enough space among the barrels of benzene to lean against the rear railing and peer out to the Atlantic Ocean. He couldn't quite see his house, but he knew exactly where it was. His wife would be up by now but the children would still be sleeping. It was cold, and the last of the nighttime fog was still lingering in patches along the harbour. The sky above was a clear blue.

Earlier Captain Le Médec had treated him to a fine French breakfast. Not his usual fare of bacon and eggs, but a new dining experience. Croissants and Brie cheese. Fresh oranges and strong coffee with thick cream. He was used to tea in the morning, but he thought he could get used to coffee, especially if it was served like this. He'd never had a croissant before, and was told that the delicacy had been invented by Napoleon for his troops in the field during his wars in Europe.

It was now just a quarter to seven, and Mackey found himself standing on the bridge with the whistle cord between him and Captain Le Médec. Glotin was beside Le Médec. Alphonse Serré stood behind them in the pilot house. There was an open space separating them, and Serré stood at the wheel awaiting orders. Mackey had made it clear to everyone that they wouldn't be sailing by charts or compass but by landmarks, using wharves, chimneys and hills as reference points.

"Are your crewmen all ready, Captain?"

"They are ready Mr. Mackey."

"There is a steamer ahead of us. As soon as it clears the examination ship and passes through the submarine nets, we have authorization to enter the outer harbour and proceed to Bedford Basin."

*   *   *

The SS *Clara* was an American tramp steamer, and as such it had no official business in Halifax. Thus, it did not fall under the Admiralty's scrutiny. Even so, it had to abide by the rules of the harbour. The pilot assigned to the SS *Clara* was 29-year-old Edward Renner. Although he had been a pilot for six years, Renner, like so many of his colleagues, often did things his own way and was sometimes handed rebukes for not following the rules.

To be fair, Renner's actions were consistent with those of the other fifteen pilots who earned a living navigating the waters of Halifax harbour. This band of brothers followed the protocols of the harbour and never questioned their existence. But these men also had worked the harbour for years. They knew its depths, its shoals and its currents. They knew from experience how fast the water ran and whether the tides worked for or against a ship. Their knowledge of the harbour told them where it was safe, and also where there were rocks that could tear out the hull of a ship in minutes.

The SS *Clara* had just cleared examination and was edging out into the outer harbour. It was just past 7:30 AM.

*   *   *

A little after 8:00 AM, as the *Mont Blanc* was casting off, twelve miles to the North the *Imo* was weighing anchor in Bedford Basin. The *Imo*'s decks were mainly empty. Most of the crew were below decks eating breakfast. The crew had just finished hauling up the anchor chains when Hayes walked onto the open bridge where Captain From was pacing the deck waiting for him. 24-year-old Johan Johansen was at the wheel. He had been to sea for several years and was quite familiar with the *Imo*.

"Good morning, Captain. You seem anxious to be on your way."

Offering a perfunctory handshake, From replied, "Good morning." He had no time for pleasantries and made no bones about his anxiety to be rid of Halifax. "We should've left yesterday. I've time to make up."

Like his friend Francis Mackey, William Hayes was a veteran harbour pilot with many years of first-hand knowledge and experience. He signaled to Johansen, "Ahead slow Mr. Helmsman. Steady as she goes." The *Imo* moved slowly forward at a leisurely two knots.

As the *Imo* approached the Narrows and was free of the Basin, Captain From gave the order: "Full speed ahead." By the time the *Imo* began the hair-pin turn to starboard she was travelling at six knots, higher than the allowed harbour speed. As she was completing her hairpin turn the SS *Clara*, sailing mid-stream, approached on the *Imo*'s port side. Hayes blasted the whistle once. The whistle was the only means that ships in the harbour had to communicate with each other.

Protocol dictated that whichever ship blasted their whistle first would control the navigation. In this case Hayes' signal blast indicated he would pass the SS *Clara* starboard to starboard. Right side to right side. The *Imo* would stay on the Dartmouth side of the harbour, not the Halifax side where it should be. They would pass starboard to starboard, against regulations. *I control the navigation because I blew the first whistle*, Hayes' conscience told him. Aboard the SS *Clara* Edward Renner answered with two blasts signaling he didn't agree with Hayes' signal and that he was going to steer for the Dartmouth shore. They would pass port to port, as protocol stipulated. He was firm in his belief.

Harbour regulations specified that ships entering and leaving the harbour must hug the shore on their starboard, or right, side. Thus, the *Imo* should have hugged the Halifax shore on its starboard side, and both ships should have passed each other port to port. The *Imo* should not have veered to the Dartmouth side, with its port side hugging the Dartmouth shore.

Hayes could have stopped the *Imo* and let the SS *Clara* pass. But because the *Imo* was a day late leaving Halifax, Captain From was determined not to brook any further delays. The ship was also travelling faster than the harbour speed limit of five knots. Hayes chose not to stop, and signaled the SS *Clara* that they would pass starboard to starboard, not port to port, as Renner had requested.

Renner was left with no choice, as the distance between the two ships was narrowing. He ordered his wheelsman to keep the SS *Clara* on the Halifax shore. The two ships managed to pass each other, starboard to starboard, without incident, but the stress level was high on both ships. As they passed close to each other, Renner, on the SS *Clara,* cupped his hands and shouted out a warning: "There is another ship following us by about twenty minutes. You may not be able to see her now because of the fog, but she is coming."

Hayes, on the open bridge of the *Imo,* did not hear the message clearly, so Renner grabbed his megaphone and repeated his message. Hayes acknowledged that he understood.

*   *   *

It was now 8:15 AM, and the *Mont Blanc* had just passed Citadel Hill, riding low in the water and moving at a snail's pace. Sailing mid-channel, Mackey was prepared to steer to starboard and pass any oncoming ships, port to port, on the left, as regulations required.

On the *Imo*, Captain From's intention was to sail midstream down the harbour and straight out to the open Atlantic. As a result of the her encounter with the SS *Clara*, the *Imo* was now much closer to the Dartmouth shore than she ought to be.

Squinting into the lingering morning mist, on the lookout for the ship Edward Renner had warned him about, Hayes saw the approaching ship far in the distance. It appeared to Hayes that the other ship, the *Mont Blanc*, was also mid-channel, in the same lane that the *Imo* was travelling, and approaching him head on. But more alarming was the sudden appearance of a tug pulling two barges filled to the hilt, leaving a Halifax dock.

*　　*　　*

To anyone working along the Halifax waterfront the *Stella Maris* was a familiar sight. The 125-foot former British gunboat and minesweeper had been converted into a tugboat and was very active on the waterfront. Today, as usual, she was captained by Horatio Brannen. Captain Brannon's 21-year old son Walter was at the wheel. The tug's duty this day was to tow two heavily laden barges filled with stone pieces to Bedford Basin.

As the *Stella Maris* pulled away from her loading dock at a sluggish four knots, the tug headed north along her normal route close to the Halifax shoreline, towards the six-story Acadia Sugar Refinery. She was pulling the two heavy barges behind her. When she reached the refinery Brannon intended to steer the *Stella Maris* to starboard and cross to the Dartmouth side of the channel. No one on board had yet noticed the *Imo*.

A few minutes later Walter was the first to spot the *Imo* through the mist bearing down on them. "Why in God's name is she travelling so fast?" he exclaimed to his startled father. "And why is she closer to the Dartmouth side?"

The *Stella Maris* had passed the refinery and was heading for the Dartmouth shore when Captain Brannon suddenly realized the critical situation he was in. His tug was travelling at a slow speed and had little maneuverability with the two barges she was towing. He could read the words BELGIAN RELIEF spelled out in block letters facing him on the starboard side of the big ship.

She was big, and travelling fast. Brannon also noted that she was light and sitting high above her water line, with her propeller sitting up in the water, making her a slow turner. He yelled to the wheelsman, "I have never seen a ship travelling that fast." He knew that there was not enough time to avoid a collision if he continued on course. "Take her into shore," he commanded his son. Walter turned sharply left to port and the safety of the Halifax shoreline.

On the deck of the *Imo* Hayes watched as the *Stella Maris* turned toward the Halifax shore. He saw no need to change course if the *Stella Maris* was going to go around him. Starboard to starboard. As he was dealing with the *Stella Maris* situation, his attention returned to the outline of the ship emerging from the morning haze less than a mile away.

"Steady to port," he shouted to the helmsman. Johansen turned the rudder slightly to the left, to port, which caused the *Imo's* bow to move in the opposite direction, to starboard, towards the Halifax side of the harbour.

Hayes was startled. He didn't realize or had forgotten that commands aboard Norwegian ships were understood differently than commands aboard ships visiting Halifax. He meant to tell Johansen to turn the ship to port. But on a Norwegian ship, if the helmsman received a command to turn to port, he would turn the rudder to port and the ship would turn to starboard, in the opposite direction.

Ships visiting English ports were supposed to follow English command rules, regardless of the rules in the ship's native country. Suddenly Hayes was faced with a situation he had not planned. The *Imo* was turning to starboard.

Hayes had wanted the *Imo* to stay closer to the Dartmouth side of the channel, where the harbour depth was more than fifty feet. Hayes knew the *Imo* was riding high in the water, and reasoned it would be safter navigating there rather than moving to starboard towards the Halifax shore. Now the *Imo* was on a collision course with the *Mont Blanc*, a half-mile away. He blasted the whistle twice to get the *Mont Blanc*'s attention. Two loud screeches echoed in the small space separating the two shores but never reached the *Mont Blanc*'s deck.

*   *   *

It was 8:30 when Francis Mackey, on the deck of *Mont Blanc*, noticed the *Stella Maris* with her two tugs in tow. Beyond the tug he could also see the two tall masts of a ship moving at speed, judging by the foam at her bow. It was those masts that kept his full attention. Recognizing the ship's profile, he knew it was the *Imo*. He had piloted her on one of her previous visits to Halifax. Mackey remained intensely aware of the *Mont Blanc*'s dangerous cargo. He also knew that without the red flag, no one in the harbour would have any inkling of the risks facing them. Especially the *Imo*. He had no hesitation in advising Captain Le Médec to proceed as slow as he possibility could.

Neither Francis Mackey nor anyone else aboard the *Mont*

Blanc had heard the *Imo*'s whistle. All of Mackey's attention was now focused on the *Imo*'s approach. He saw the Norwegian ship turning right from the Dartmouth side of the channel moving at speed toward them. The *Imo* was cutting across the *Mont Blanc*'s intended path. Unless the *Imo* changed course there was going to be a collision.

Mackey was furious. He knew that Hayes, a friend and veteran pilot, was supposed to be piloting the *Imo* through the harbour today, but he wondered if that was really Hayes on the *Imo*'s bridge. Mackey raged, "Look at that damn fool coming into our water! He should stay on the Dartmouth side of the channel."

Mackey was confident the *Mont Blanc* was where she was supposed to be in the harbour channel. The ship continued to proceed at a crawl. Mackey was so sure that he had the right-of-way that he gave the whistle one sharp pull. "I hope he understands that I am signalling to gain his attention," he said, "and that he should get out of our way." He considered his whistle to be the first communication between the vessels.

He hoped that Hayes was indeed the pilot aboard the *Imo*, and that he would heed this warning that the *Mont Blanc* had the right-of-way. Just to be cautious, Mackey issued Le Médec new orders. "Dead slow. And take her a little to starboard." He wanted to be out of the way if the *Imo* continued on its trajectory toward the Halifax side.

Mackey also wanted to put as much distance between the *Mont Blanc* and the *Imo* as possible, and he was willing to risk sailing the *Mont Blanc* closer to the Dartmouth shore to do that. The two ships would pass port to port.

On the bridge of the *Imo*, William Hayes heard the single blast of the *Mont Blanc*'s whistle. He was puzzled by the single blast. He thought it was a response to his first signal, when in fact it was not. Hayes gave two blasts of the *Imo*'s whistle, meaning he was going to port. He thought the *Mont Blanc* intended to stay on the Halifax side of the channel, the same as the *Stella Maris* had done. That was his thinking, and he felt he had no choice but to believe that that was the case. He ordered Captain From to turn the *Imo*'s helm to port. Towards Dartmouth.

The *Mont Blanc* was just passing a grouping of wharves adjacent to the refinery. The wharves were packed with ships, including the naval tug *Neried*. Its commander, John Makiny, looked up at the sound of the double whistle and saw the *Imo* turning to port. He knew that the double blast was an incorrect call. The *Imo* should have deferred to the *Mont Blanc*, as required by law, and turned to starboard, towards the Halifax shore. They should have lined up to pass port to port. It was evident to Makiny that the French ship was clearly in her correct lane and the Norwegian ship was not. He called out to his crew, "Come out here and watch this! There's going to be a head-on collision."

The *Mont Blanc* was now close to the Dartmouth shore and running out of room to maneuver. The *Imo* and the *Month Blanc* were only a ship's length apart. Mackey knew he could not risk grounding the ship for fear of setting off the explosives. He had no alternative but to cross the harbour against regulations, and he had to do so immediately. "Bear hard to port!" he hollered. Serré desperately spun the wheel and the *Mont Blanc* turned left towards the Halifax shore.

The *Imo* had stopped her engines, but her momentum was still carrying her forward. By some miracle, Mackey's efforts worked. The two ships ended up bow to bow with only 55 yards between them. Starboard to starboard. Mackey gripped the nearest handrail and let out a deep sigh, "We made it!"

But it wasn't meant to be. Fate had other plans. The *Mont Blanc* had also stopped her engines, which were now idling, but the ship still kept its forward momentum towards the bow of the *Imo*.

Hayes, on the *Imo*'s deck, could see no way to avoid a collision. Instinctively he grabbed furiously at the ship's telegraph handle in the faint hope his signal to the engine room to reverse the *Imo*'s engines would be in time. But it was too late.

Without any cargo the *Imo* was riding high in the water, so high as to render her propeller useless. Reversing the *Imo*'s engines was a disaster. It created a reverse thrust, which pointed the *Imo*'s bow perpendicular to the *Mont Blanc*'s bow.

Mackey and Le Médec stood on the bridge of the *Mont Blanc*, staring in shock as the *Imo* skimmed across the water directly at their hull. All they could do was brace for the impact.

The *Imo*'s port bow, with its dangling anchor, plowed into the *Mont Blanc* with a terrible screeching cry of wrenched metal. The *Imo* pushed ten feet into the hold, barely missing Hold #2, where the TNT was stored. The collision created a shock wave that travelled through both ships, just as if they had made a hard landing at a wharf. The noise alerted everyone near the waterfront of the unfolding crisis.

At the same time, the *Imo*'s engines had fully engaged, and with a roar of tearing metal the *Imo* reversed at full speed. Despite the warning screams of the sailors aboard the *Mont Blanc*, they could not stop the *Imo*'s reverse action.

To make matters worse, the *Imo*'s bow anchor had become tangled in the *Mont Blanc*'s superstructure, and was straining against immense pressure to keep the two ships from separating. Finally, with a sickening screech of whining metal the *Imo* jerked free. As the *Imo*'s anchor was wrenched free, it took with it part of the steel plating that protected the *Mont Blanc*'s hold. The sudden force of the *Imo*'s separation sent the *Mont Blanc* pivoting towards the Halifax shore. Its bow was now aimed directly at Pier 8.

As they drifted towards the Halifax shore, Mackey leaned over the starboard rail to inspect the damage. He said in a hopeful voice, "Captain, I can see that she is open from the waterline to the deck. She is not taking on water. And, good news, I can see no fire. Not even any smoke. If we are careful, we should be able to get through this."

"If God is on our side, Mr. Mackey. If he is watching over us."

Unbeknownst to either the pilot or the captain, the collision had released a few dry grains of highly combustible picric, which were now starting to smolder. It was 8:40 AM.

* * *

The pulse of Halifax was beating normally on this Thursday morning. Except for professionals like lawyers and bankers, most people were already at work. Shopkeepers had opened for business. Schoolkids were already in their classrooms, or on their way. Delivery vehicles, propelled by both gasoline and horse, were going about their business already, clogging the lower streets along the waterfront. Workers at the dockyard and the refinery had long been at their jobs. Because it was market day, many hay wagons also filled the streets.

Over on Pier 8 Ben and Danny were helping a stevedore gang load pallets of medical supplies onto an English cargo ship. It was always a hectic time in the days before convoys were preparing to set sail. The waterfront was teeming with dockyard workers.

"What the hell was that?" Ben yelled to no one in particular."

"Two ships just rammed each other," someone yelled. "It looks like they're on fire." People started to push, shoving their way forward for a good vantage point at the pier's edge. Ben and Danny made it to the front row, but were so hemmed in they were afraid of being pushed into the water. They could see flames engulfing the ship, shooting fifty feet into the air and billowing thick black smoke.

The ship Ben was staring at, along with hundreds of curious onlookers who lined the waterfront docks for this spectacular entertainment, was the *Mont Blanc*. The ship was pointed across the shipping channels and drifting towards Pier 8. They could see smoking barrels being tossed high up into the air. The unfolding tragedy held everyone's attention.

Most of the spectators didn't fear an explosion. Most thought from the smell that the ship was carrying petroleum, which was a common cargo in these war years. Fires like that usually burned themselves out, or the ships were sunk by harbour authorities if there was a heightened risk. There was no red warning flag on the ship to alert anyone to the looming danger.

Sailors on the deck of the *Imo* were also unaware that the *Mont Blanc* was carrying explosives.

"What cargo do you think that French ship is carrying? I hope it's not explosives."

"No, it's probably case oil or gasoline. If it were explosives, she'd be flying the red warning flag."

*   *   *

Within a few minutes of Mackey making his initial inspection, escaping benzol vapours from ruptured barrels on deck began drifting into the holds below. When they reached the smoldering picric acid, they immediately burst into flame. Within minutes, the fire was out of control and had engulfed the entire starboard side of the *Mont Blanc*. Fireballs shot high up into the blue sky accompanied by thick black smoke. Loud *whumps* could be heard periodically as barrels exploded and were flung up into the cloudless sky.

Sailors, driven back to the foredeck by the rapidly spreading flames, clustered below the bridge awaiting orders to abandon ship. They were understandably very anxious, knowing that the hold below their feet carried enough TNT to blast everyone on board and everyone within a mile or two to kingdom come. Complete destruction. It was a fearsome fate to ponder. Le Médec turned to Mackey: "Is there anything that can be done?"

Mackey was ready with his answer. He had already assessed their options. They could not lower their anchor because they were cut off by the fire and could not reach the capstan. There was no way of getting water into the hold. He knew the ship was doomed. Approaching fireboats racing to help the *Mont Blanc* saw frantically waving sailors as a call for help, not as a warning.

Le Médec knew the impossibility of trying to warn the people lining the waterfront of the impending disaster. His heart was bursting with dread.

"Abandon ship." Le Médec gave the order to his First Officer. "Man the lifeboats." If he couldn't save anyone on shore, he could at least save his crew.

After the *Mont Blanc* had departed New York, as a precaution they had lowered their lifeboats to launch position. Crew members needed no urging. Lifeboats were lowered in an orderly fashion. There was no panic, and in less than five minutes most of the crew had departed the ship. They desperately rowed towards the Dartmouth shore, which was the closest land within reach.

Le Médec and Mackey were still on the bridge, along with First Officer Glotin and Serré, the wheelsman.

"Set the helm amidships," ordered Le Médec. It was the captain's last effort to keep the *Mont Blanc* from drifting into the Halifax docks.

Serré quickly straightened the wheel, pointing the ship towards the middle of the shipping channel. He locked the wheel in place and bolted down the stairs to the lifeboats.

Glotin and Mackey slid down the ropes to the lower deck. Le Médec remained at the top of the ladder. He was determined to go down with the ship. He was responsible for this disaster. *It's the right thing to do*, he thought.

An exasperated Glotin climbed back up to the deck and roughly took hold of Le Médec by the arm and shoulder. Mackey couldn't understand their heated conversation, because it was entirely in French. He later learned that Glotin had convinced the captain that his sacrifice was unnecessary, as all the crew were safe. He had assured Le Médec that staying on board would be useless, and there was no need for him to die. Something Glotin said managed to calm Le Médec, who reluctantly followed him down the ladder.

Once in the lifeboats, Mackey took charge. "The ship is going to explode very soon. We have to get as far away as possible." He pointed toward the ferry dock in Turtle Cove, nestled into the northern shoreline of Dartmouth. He waved frantically to the other lifeboats to follow him to safety. "The forest is thick there, which will offer us some protection."

* * *

Fort Needham sat atop a high hill, looking straight down Richmond Street to the harbour. The hill was thronged with curious spectators watching the burning ship directly below them.

There was almost a festive air exciting the crowd. They could see along the waterfront, where many people had climbed onto roofs to witness the spectacle.

On Pier 8, Ben Stent was growing concerned about the oily smoke that was reaching the pier. As he turned to leave his vantage point, he glanced one last time at the burning ship. The bomb that was the *Mont Blanc* exploded. His brain did not register the event because he ceased to exist before the blast reached his consciousness.

It was precisely 9:04 AM.

More than a thousand people were killed instantly by the powerful heat wave created by the explosion. The force of the air pressure travelled so fast it slammed into the side of Citadel Hill, where it was deflected high up into the atmosphere. Lucky for those who lived south of the hill.

An immense tidal wave immediately followed the blast and swept another thousand people out to sea. The tidal wave reached three streets up into the city and cleared everything in its path. Most bodies were never recovered.

After the noise of the explosion ceased there was a profound silence. A momentary pause before the cries of agony engulfed the shattered city.

64

7 December 1917. Halifax.

ON THE SAME DAY AS THE *MONT BLANC* EXPLODED, another devasting bomb was being created. Cold arctic air was meeting warm moist air off the coast of North Carolina. Some called this phenomenon an Eastern Seaboard bomb, because it dumped so much snow so fast. It was headed directly up the coast, to Nova Scotia.

During Thursday night the temperature in Halifax dropped twenty degrees Fahrenheit, to sixteen degrees. In the late evening and throughout the night it snowed. And snowed. And continued to snow until Friday mid-morning, when Halifax found itself encased in a fierce blizzard. Gale force winds of 45 miles an hour ravaged the already shattered city.

Amid the wreckage of Fort Needham, Harry looked down onto the pinched part of the harbour that was the Narrows. Everywhere he looked he could see, through the thick covering of snow, the blackness, death and destruction. Evil peeked out of hiding places, like it was afraid to acknowledge the carnage that befell this city. He could smell the smoke and stench that still escaped the city's black wounds.

He wondered about God. He thought about all the old excuses. He asked himself, "Could a just and loving God allow this to happen? Would God permit this evil manifestation to thrive?" He had heard the meaningless apologies countless times. *God works in mysterious ways. It is God's will.* Harry knew the religious response would be, "Let us pray." *No comfort there*, he thought.

Maybe it was the loss of the station house on the side of Citadel Hill, swept away with Mike Gallagher and the rest of the on-duty policemen. Harry could not explain to himself any acceptable answer that made sense. All he could see was that stained snow mantel, and think that maybe that was God's way of covering up his own sins.

Acknowledgements

I would foremost like to thank my editor and designer, David Edelstein, for turning my manuscript into a novel.

And thank you, Kent Baker, for being my mentor.